EXILES OF THE STARS

Andre Norton

As crew members of the Free Trader ship *Lydis*, Maelen, in the furred body of Vors, and Krip Vorlund, who now walked as a Thassa, had put down on the planet Thoth to find themselves in the midst of an explosive civil war. The Thothian priests wanted them to transport the valuable Forerunner treasure to Ptah for safekeeping. The Free Traders agreed, but shortly after lift-off a sudden power failure forced their ship down on the uninhabited planet of Sekhmet.

How and why the *Lydis* was marooned was a mystery which neither Krip, with his esper powers, nor Maelen, with all the talents and knowledge granted her in her life as a Moon Singer, could penetrate. Their exploration of Sekhmet compounded the mystery, threatening to extinguish the identity of the searchers themselves—for the barren planet was not deserted after all. An underground labyrinth held in stass-freeze an army of aliens, and the bodies of four beings wearing the diadems of Set, Thoth, Ptah, and the cat goddess Sekhmet. They seemed to be the source of awesome powers—power able to run machinery by remote mental control or to commandeer the bodies of men, power which emanated from a time beyond the memory of man.

In this sequel to *Moon of Three Rings*, Andre Norton has created a fantasy–adventure story with the skilled imagination of a master writer of science fiction.

Exiles of the Stars

Also by Andre Norton

Ice Crown
Uncharted Stars
The Zero Stone
Moon of Three Rings
Quest Crosstime

Exiles
of the Stars

Andre Norton

THE VIKING PRESS   NEW YORK

First Edition
Copyright © 1971 by Andre Norton
All rights reserved
First published in 1971 by The Viking Press, Inc.
625 Madison Avenue, New York, N.Y. 10022
Published simultaneously in Canada by
The Macmillan Company of Canada Limited
Library of Congress catalog card number: 72–136817
Printed in U.S.A.
Fic   1. Science fiction

Trade 670–30112–4   VLB 670–30113–2
  1   2   3   4   5   75   74   73   72   71

Exiles of the Stars

Chapter 1

KRIP VORLUND

There was an odd haze in the room, or was it my eyes? I cupped my hands over them for a moment as I wondered, not only about trusting in my sight, but about this whole situation. For the haze might be the visible emanation of that emotion anyone with the slightest esper talent could pick up clearly—the acrid taste, touch, smell, of fear. Not our own fear, but that of the city which pulsed around us like the uneven breathing of a great terrified animal.

Sensing that, I wanted to run out of the room, the building, beyond the city walls to such security as the *Lydis* had to offer, where the shell of the Free Trader which was my home could shut out that aura of a fear fast approaching panic. Yet I sat where I was, forced my hands to lie quietly across my knees as I watched those in the room with me, listened to the clicking speech of the men of Kartum on the planet Thoth.

There were four of them. Two were priests, both past middle life, both of high standing by the richness of their deep-violet over-mantles, which they had not put aside even though the room was far too warm. The dark skin of their faces, shaven heads, and gesturing hands was lightened with designs in ceremonial yellow paint. Each fingernail was covered with a claw-shaped metal sheath set with tiny gems, which winked and blinked even in this subdued lighting as their fingers, flickering in and out, drew symbols in the air as if they could not carry on any serious conversation without the constant invocation of their god.

Their companions were officials of the ruler of Kartum, as close to him, they averred in the speech of Thoth, as the hairs of his ceremonial royal beard. They sat across the table from our captain, Urban Foss, seemingly willing enough to let the priests do the talking. But their hands were never far from weapon butts, as if they expected at any moment to see the door burst open, the enemy in upon us.

There were three of us from the *Lydis*—Captain Foss, cargomaster Juhel Lidj, and me, Krip Vorlund, the least of that company—Free Traders, born to space and the freedom of the starways as are all our kind. We have been rovers for so long that we have perhaps mutated into a new breed of humankind. Nothing to us, these planet intrigues —not unless we were entrapped in them. And that did not happen often. Experience, a grim teacher, had made us very wary of the politics of the planet-born.

Three—no, we were four. I dropped a hand now and my fingers touched a stiff brush of upstanding hair. I did not have to glance down to know what—who—sat up on her haunches beside my chair, feeling, sensing even more strongly than I the unease of spirit, the creeping menace which darkened about us.

Outwardly there was a glassia of Yiktor there, black-furred except for the tuft of coarse, stiffened gray-white bristles on the crown of the head, with a slender tail as long again as the body, and large paws with sheathed, dagger-sharp claws. Yet appearances were deceiving. For the animal body housed another spirit. This was truly Maelen —she once a Moon Singer of the Thassa—who had been given this outer shape when her own body was broken and dying, then was condemned by her own people to its wearing because she had broken their laws.

Yiktor of the three-ringed moon— What had happened there more than a planet-year ago was printed on my mind so that no small detail could ever be forgotten. It was Maelen who had saved me—my life if not my body, or the body I had worn when I landed there. That body was long since "dead"—spaced to drift forever among the stars— unless it be drawn some day into the fiery embrace of a sun and consumed.

I had had a second body, one which had run on four legs, hunted and killed, bayed at the moon Sotrath—which left in my mind strange dreams of a world which was all scent and sounds such as my own species never knew. And now I wore a third covering, akin to the first and yet different, a body which had another small residue of the alien to creep slowly into my consciousness, so that at times even the world of the *Lydis* (which I had known from birth) seemed strange, a little distorted. Yet I was Krip Vorlund in truth, no matter what outer covering I might wear (that now being the husk of Maquad of the Thassa). Maelen had done this—the twice changing—and for that, despite her motives of good, not ill—she went now four-footed, furred, in my company. Not that I regretted the last.

I had been first a man, then a barsk, and was now outwardly a Thassa; and parts of all mingled in me. My fingers moved through Maelen's stiff crest as I listened, watched, sucked in air tainted not only with queer odors peculiar to a house of Kartum but with the emotions of its inhabitants. I had always possessed the talent of mind-seek. Many Traders developed that, so it was not uncommon. But I also knew that in Maquad's body such a sense had been heightened, sharpened. That was why I was one of this company at this hour, my superiors valuing my worth as an esper to judge those we must deal with.

And I knew that Maelen's even keener powers must also be at work, weighing, assaying. With our combined report Foss would have much on which to base his decision. And that decision must come very soon.

The *Lydis* had planeted four days ago with a routine cargo of pulmn, a powder made from the kelp beds of Hawaika. In ordinary times that powder would have been sold to the temples to become fuel for their ever-burning scented fires. The trade was not a fabulously handsome payload, but it made a reasonable profit. And there was to be picked up in return (if one got on the good side of the priests) the treasures of Nod—or a trickle of them. Which in turn were worth very much indeed on any inner world.

Thoth, Ptah, Anubis, Sekhmet, Set; five planets with the sun Amen-Re to warm them. Of the five, Set was too close to that sun to support life, Anubis a frozen waste without colonization. Which left Thoth, Ptah, and Sekhmet. All those had been explored, two partly colonized, generations

ago, by Terran-descended settlers. Only those settlers had
not been the first.

Our kind is late come to space; that we learned on our
first galactic voyaging. There have been races, empires,
which rose, fell, and vanished long before our ancestors
lifted their heads to wonder dimly at the nature of the stars.
Wherever we go we find traces of these other peoples—
though there is much we do not know, cannot learn. "Forerunners" we call them, lumping them all together. Though
more and more we are coming to understand that there
were many more than just one such galaxy-wide empire, one
single race voyaging in the past. But we have learned so
little.

The system of Amen-Re turned out to be particularly rich
in ancient remains. But it was not known yet whether the
civilization which had flourished here had been only system-
wide, or perhaps an outpost of a yet-unclassified galactic
one. Mainly because the priests had very early taken upon
themselves the guardianship of such "treasure."

Each people has its gods, its controlling powers. There is
an inner need in our species to acknowledge something beyond ourselves, something greater. In some civilizations
there is a primitive retrogression to sacrifice—even of the
worshipers' own kind—and to religions of fear and darkness.
Or belief can be the recognition of a spirit, without any
formal protestation of rites. But on many worlds the gods
are strong and their voices, the priests, are considered in-
fallible, above even the temporal rulers. So that Traders
walk softly and cautiously on any world where there are
many temples and such a priesthood.

The system of Amen-Re had been colonized by ships

from Veda. And those had been filled with refugees from a
devastating religious war—the persecuted, fleeing. Thus a
hierarchy had had control from the first.

Luckily they were not rigidly fanatical toward the unknown. On some worlds the remnants of any native former
civilization were destroyed as devilish work. But in the case
of Amen-Re some farsighted high priest in the early days
had had the wit to realize that these remains were indeed
treasure which could be exploited. He had proclaimed all
such finds the due of the god, to be kept in the temples.

When Traders began to call at Thoth (settlement on
Ptah was too small to induce visits), lesser finds were offered
in bargaining, and these became the reason for cargo exploi-
tation. For there was no other local product on Thoth
worth the expense of off-world shipping.

It was the lesser bits, the crumbs, which were so offered.
The bulk of the best was used to adorn the temples. But
those were enough to make the trip worthwhile for my people, if not for the great companies and combines. Our cargo
space was strictly limited; we lived on the fringe of the trade
of the galaxy, picking up those items too small to entice the
bigger dealers.

So trade with Thoth had become routine. But ship time
is not planet time. Between one visit and the next there
may be a vast change on any world, political or even physical. And when the Lydis had set down this time, she had
found boiling around her the beginnings of chaos, unless
there came some sharp change. Government, religion, do
not exist in a vacuum. Here government and religion—
which had always had a firm alliance—were together under
fire.

A half year earlier there had arisen in the mountain country to the east of Kartum a new prophet. There had been such before, but somehow the temples had managed either to discredit them or to absorb their teachings without undue trouble. This time the priesthood found itself on the defensive. And, its complacency well established by years of untroubled rule, it handled the initial difficulty clumsily.

As sometimes happens, one mistake led to a greater, until now the government at Kartum was virtually in a state of siege. With the church under pressure, the temporal powers scented independence. The well-established nobility was loyal to the temple. After all, their affairs were so intertwined that they could not easily withdraw their support. But there are always have-nots wanting to be haves—lesser nobility and members of old families who resent not having more. And some of these made common cause with the rebels.

The spark which had set it off was the uncovering of a "treasure" place which held some mysterious contagion swift to kill off those involved. Not only that, but the plague spread, bringing death to others who had not dealt with the place at all. Then a fanatical hill priest-prophet began to preach that the treasures were evil and should be destroyed.

He led a mob to blow up the infected site, then went on, hot with the thirst for destruction, to do the same to the local temple which served as a storage place for the goods. The authorities moved in then, and the contagion attacked the troops. This was accepted by the surviving rebels as a vindication of their beliefs. So the uprising spread, finding adherents who wanted nothing more than to upset the status quo.

As is only too common where there has been an un-troubled rule, the authorities had not realized the serious-ness of what they termed a local outburst. There had been quite a few among the higher-placed priests and nobles who had been loath to move at once, wanting to conciliate the rebels. In fact there had been too much talk and not enough action at just the wrong moment.

Now there was a first-class civil war in progress. And, as far as we were able to learn, the government was shaky. Which was the reason for this secret meeting here in the house of a local lordling. The *Lydis* had come in with a cargo now of little or no value. And while a Free Trader may make an unpaying voyage once, a second such can put the ship in debt to the League.

To be without a ship is death for my kind. We know no other life—planetside existence is prison. And even if we could scrape a berth on another Trader, that would mean starting from the bottom once again, with little hope of ever climbing to freedom again. It would perhaps not be so hard on junior members of the crew, such as myself, who was only assistant cargomaster. But we had had to fight for even our lowly berths. As for Captain Foss, the other officers —it would mean total defeat.

Thus, though we had learned of the upsetting state of affairs within a half hour after landing, we did not space again. As long as there was the least hope of turning the voyage to some account we remained finned down, even though we were sure there was presently no market for pulmn. As a matter of routine, Foss and Lidj had contacted the temple. But instead of our arranging an open meeting with a supply priest, they had summoned us here.

So great was their need that they wasted no time in formal greeting but came directly to the point. For it seemed that after all we did have something to sell—safety. Not for the men who met us, nor even for their superiors, but for the cream of the planet's treasure, which could be loaded on board the *Lydis* and sent to protective custody elsewhere.

On Ptah the temple had established a well-based outpost, mainly because certain minerals were mined there. And it had become a recognized custom for the hierarchy of the church to withdraw to Ptah at times for periods of retreat, removed from the distractions of Thoth. It was to that sanctuary that they proposed now to send the pick of the temple holdings, and the *Lydis* was to transport them.

When Captain Foss asked why they did not use their own ore-transport ships for the purpose (not that he was averse to the chance to make this trip pay), they had a quick answer. First, the ore ships were mainly robo-controlled, not prepared to carry a crew of more than one or two techs on board. They could not risk sending the treasure in such, when tinkering with the controls might lose it forever. Secondly, the *Lydis*, being a Free Trader, could be trusted. For such was the Traders' reputation that all knew, once under contract, we held by our word. To void such a bond was unthinkable. The few, very few, times it had happened, the League itself had meted out such punishment as we did not care to remember.

Therefore, they said, if we took contract they knew that their cargo would be delivered. And not only one such cargo, but they would have at least two, maybe more. If the rebels did not invest the city(as they now threatened) too soon, the priests would continue to send off their hoard as

long as they could. But the cream of it all would be on the
first trip. And they would pay—which was the subject of
the present meeting.

Not that we were having any wrangling. But no man be-
comes a Trader without a very shrewd idea of how to judge
his wares or services. Thus to out-bargain one of us was
virtually impossible. And, too, this was a seller's market, and
we had a monopoly on what we had to offer.

There had been two serious defeats of the government
forces within a matter of ten days. Though the loyal army
still stubbornly held the road to the city, there was no reason to believe that they could continue to do so for long. So
Foss and Lidj made the best of their advantage. There was
also the danger of an uprising in Kartum, as three other
cities had already fallen to rebels working from within, in-
citing mobs to violence and taking advantage of such out-
bursts. As one of the priests had said, it was almost as if a
kind of raging insanity spread from man to man at these
times.

"Trouble—" I did not need that mind-alert from Maelen,
for I could feel it also, an ingathering of darkness, as if any
light was being swallowed up by shadows. Whether the
priests had any esper talents, I did not know. Perhaps even
this aura of panic could be induced by a gifted enemy at
work. Though I did not pick up any distinct trace of such
interference.

I stirred; Lidj glanced at me, picked up my unspoken
warning. Those of the *Lydis* had learned, even as I, that
since my return to the ship in this Thassa body my esper
powers were greater than they had once been. In turn he
nodded at the priests.

"Let it be so contracted." As cargomaster he had the final decision. For in such matters he could overrule even the captain. Trade was his duty, first and always.

But if the priests were relieved, there was no lightening of the tension in that chamber. Maelen pressed against my knee, but she did not mind-touch. Only I noted that her head tuft was no longer so erect. And I remembered of old that the sign of anger or alarm with the glassia was a flattening of that tuft to lie against the skull. So I sent mind-seek swiftly to probe the atmosphere.

Straight mind-to-mind reading cannot be unless it is willed by both participants. But it is easy enough to tune in on emotions, and I found (though at a distance which I could not measure) something which sent my hand to the butt of my stunner, even as Maelen's crest had betrayed her own concern. There was menace far more directed than the uneasiness in this room. But I could not read whether it was directed against those who had summoned us, or against our own ship's party.

The priests left first with the nobles. They had guardsmen waiting without—which we had not. Foss looked directly to me.

"Something is amiss, more than just the general situation," he commented.

"There is trouble waiting out there." I nodded to the door and what lay beyond. "Yes, more than what we might ordinarily expect."

Maelen reared, setting her forepaws against me, her head raised so that her golden eyes looked into mine. Her thought was plain in my mind.

"Let me go first. A scout is needed."

I was loath to agree. Here she was plainly alien and, as such, might not only attract unwelcome attention but, in the trigger-set tension, even invite attack.

"Not so." She had read my thought. "You forget—it is night. And I, being in this body, know how to use the dark as a friend."

So I opened the door and she slipped through. The hall without was not well lighted and I marveled at how well she used the general dusk as a cover, being gone before I was aware. Foss and Lidj joined me, the captain saying, "There is a very wrong feel here. The sooner we raise ship, I am thinking, the better. How long will loading take?"

Lidj shrugged. "That depends upon the bulk of the cargo. At any rate we can make all ready to handle it." He spoke in code into his wrist com, giving orders to dump the pulmn to make room. There was this much the priests had had to agree to—they must let us, at the other end of the voyage, take our reckoning out of the treasure already stored in the temple on Ptah. And a certain amount must be in pieces of our own selection. Usually Traders had to accept discards without choice.

We headed for the street. By Foss's precaution our meeting had been held in a house close to the city wall, so we need not venture far into Kartum. But I, for one, knew that I would not breathe really easily again until my boot plates rang on the *Lydis's* entry ramp. The dusk which had hung at our coming had thickened into night. But there was still the roar of life in the city.

Then—

" 'Ware!" Maelen's warning was as sharp as a vocal shout. "Make haste for the gates!"

She had sent with such power that even Foss had picked up her alert, and I did not need to pass her message on. We started at a trot for the gate, Foss getting out our entry pass.

I noticed a flurry by that barrier as we neared. Fighting. Above the hoarse shouting of the men milling in combat came the *crack* of the native weapons. Luckily this was not a planet which dealt with lasers or blasters. But they had solid-projectile weapons which made a din. Our stunners could not kill, only render unconscious. But we could die from one of those archaic arms in use ahead as quickly as from a blaster.

Foss adjusted the beam button of his stunner; Lidj and I did likewise, altering from narrow ray to wide sweep. Such firing exhausted the charges quickly, but in such cases as this we had no choice. We must clear a path ahead.

"To the right—" Lidj did not really need that direction from Foss. He had already moved into flank position on one side, as I did on the other.

We hurried on, knowing that we must get closer for a most effective attack. Then I saw Maelen hunkered in a doorway. She ran to me, ready to join our final dash.

"Now!"

We fired together, sweeping all the struggling company, friend and foe alike, if we did have friends among those fighters. Men staggered and fell, and we began to run, leaping over the prone bodies sprawled across the gate opening. But the barrier itself was closed and we thrust against it in vain.

"Lever, in the gatehouse—" panted Foss.

Maelen streaked away. She might no longer have humanoid hands, but glassia paws are not to be underesti-

mated. And that she was able to make good use of those
she demonstrated a moment later as the side panels drew
back to let us wriggle through.

Then we ran as if the demon hosts of Nebu brayed at our
heels. For at any moment one of those projectile weapons
might be aimed at us. I, for one, felt a strange sensation
between my shoulder blades, somehow anticipating such a
wound.

However, there came no such stroke of ill fortune, and
we did reach the ramp and safety. So all four of us, Maelen
running with the greatest ease, pounded up into the *Lydis*.
And we were hardly through the hatch opening when we
heard the grate of metal, knew that those on duty were sealing the ship.

Foss leaned against the wall by the ramp, thumbing a
new charge into his stunner. It was plain that from now on
we must be prepared to defend ourselves, as much as if we
were on an openly hostile world.

I looked to Maelen. "Did you warn of the fight at the
gate?"

"Not so. There were those a-prowl who sought to capture
you. They would prevent the treasure from going hence.
But they came too late. And I think that the gate fight, in
a manner, spoiled their plans."

Foss had not followed that, so I reported it to him.

He was grimly close-faced now. "If we are to raise that
treasure—they will have to send it to us. No man from here
goes planetside again!"

Chapter 2

KRIP VORLUND

"So, what do we do now? We're safe enough in the ship. But how long do we wait?" Manus Hunold, our astrogator, had triggered the visa-plate, and we who had crowded into the control cabin to watch by its aid what happened without were intent on what it could show us.

Men streamed out onto the field, ringing in the *Lydis*—though they showed a very healthy regard for her blast-off rockets and kept a prudent distance from the lift area near her fins. They were not of the half-soldier, half-police force who supported authority, though they were armed and even kept a ragged discipline in their confrontation of the ship. However, how they could expect to come to any open quarrel with us if we stayed inside, I could not guess.

I had snapped mind-seek; there were too many waves of raw emotion circling out there. To tune to any point in that sea of violence was to tax my power near to burn-out.

"They can't be stupid enough to believe they can overrun us—" That was Pawlin Shallard, our engineer. "They're too far above the primitive to think that possible."

"No." Lidj had his head up, was watching the screen so intently he might be trying to pick out of that crowd some certain face or figure. Hunold had set the screen on "circle" as he might have done at a first set-down on an unexplored world, so that the scene shifted, allowing us a slow survey about the landing site. "No, they won't rush us. They want something else. To prevent our cargo from coming. But these are city men—I would not have believed the rebels had infiltrated in such numbers or so quickly—" He broke off, frowning at the ever-changing picture.

"Wait!" Foss pushed a "hold" button and that slow revolution was halted.

What we saw now was the gate through which we had come only a short time ago. Through it was issuing a well-armed force in uniform, the first sign of a disciplined attack on the rebels. The men in it spread out as skirmishers to form a loose cover for a cart. On that was mounted a long-snouted, heavy-looking tube which men swung down and around to face the mob between them and the ship. A fringe of the rebels began to push away from the line of fire. But that great barrel swung in a small arc, as if warning of the swath it could cut through their ranks.

Men ran from the mass of those besieging us—first by ones and twos, and then by squads. We had no idea of the more complex weapons of Thoth, but it would seem that this was one the natives held in high respect. The mob was not giving up entirely. But the ranks of the loyal soldiery were being constantly augmented from the city, pushing out and out, the mob retreating sullenly before them.

"This is it!" Lidj made for the ship ladder. "I'd say they are going to run the cargo out now. Do we open to load?"

Under normal circumstances the loading of the ship was his department. But with the safety of the *Lydis* perhaps at stake, that decision passed automatically to Foss.

"Cover the hatches with stunners; open the upper first. Until we see how well they manage—" was the captain's answer.

Minutes later we stood within the upper hatch. It was open and I had an unpleasantly naked feeling as I waited at my duty post, my calculator fastened to my wrist instead of lying in the palm of my hand, leaving me free to use my weapon. This time I had that set on narrow beam. Griss Sharvan, second engineer, pressed into guard service and facing me on the other side of the cargo opening, kept his ready on high-energy spray.

The barreled weapon had been moved farther out, to free the city gate. But its snout still swung in a jerky pattern, right to left and back again. There were no members of the mob left in front of us within the now-narrowed field of our vision, except several prone bodies, men who must have been picked off by the skirmishers.

Beyond, the gate had been opened to its furthest extent. And through that gap came the first of the heavily loaded transports. The Thothians had motorized cars which burned liquid fuel. To us such seemed sluggish when compared to the solar-energized machines of the inner planets. But at least they were better than the animal-drawn vehicles of truly primitive worlds. And now three of these trucks crawled over the field toward the *Lydis*.

A robed priest drove each, but there were guards aboard, on the alert, their heads protected by grotesque bowl-shaped helmets, their weapons ready. Between those, we saw, as the first truck ground nearer, more priests crouched behind what small protection the sides of the vehicles offered, their faces livid. But they arose quickly as the truck came to a halt under the swinging lines of our crane, and pawed at the top boxes and bales of the cargo. It seemed that they were to shift that while the guards remained on the defensive.

Thus began the loading of the *Lydis*. The priests were willing but awkward workers. So I swung out and down with the crane to help below, trying not to think of the possibility of a lucky shot from the mob. For there was the crackle of firing now coming from a distance.

Up and down, in with the crane ropes, up—down. We had to use great care, for though all were well muffled in wrappings, we knew that what we handled were irreplaceable treasures. The first truck, emptied, drew to one side. But the men who had manned it remained, the priests to help with the loading of the next, the guards spreading out as had the skirmishers from the gate. I continued to supervise the loading, at the same time listing the number of each piece swung aloft, reciting it into my recorder. Lidj by the hatch would be making a duplicate of my record, and together they would be officially sealed in the presence of the priests' representatives when all was aboard.

Three trucks we emptied. The load of the fourth consisted of only four pieces—one extra-large, three small. I signaled for double crane power, not quite sure if the biggest crate could be maneuvered through the hatch. It was a tight squeeze, but the men there managed it. When I saw it disappear I spoke to the priest in charge.

"Any more?"

He shook his head as he still watched where that large crate had vanished. Then he looked to me.

"No more. But the High One will come to take receipt for the shipment."

"How soon?" I pressed. Still I did not use mind-touch. There was too much chance of being overwhelmed by the raw emotion engendered on a battlefield. Of course the *Lydis* was such a fort as could not be stormed, but I knew the sooner we raised from Thoth the better.

"When he can." His answer was ambiguous enough to be irritating. Already he turned away, calling some order in the native tongue.

I shrugged and swung up to the hatch. There was a stowage robo at work there. My superior leaned against the wall just inside, reading the dial of his recorder. As I came in he pressed the "stop" button to seal off his list.

"They won't take receipt," I reported. "They say that there is a High One coming to do that."

Lidj grunted, so I went to see to the sealing of the holds. The large crate which had been the last was still in the claws of two robo haulers. And, strong as those were, it was not easily moved. I watched them center it in the smaller top hold, snap on the locks to keep it in position during flight. That was the last, and I could now slide the doors shut, imprint the seal which would protect the cargo until we planeted once more. Of course Lidj would be along later to add his thumb signature to mine, and only when the two of us released it could anything less than a destruct burner get it out.

I stopped in my cabin as I went aloft. Maelen, as was usual during cargo loading, lay on her own bunk there. Her crested head rested on her two forepaws, which were folded under her muzzle as she stretched out at her ease. But she was not sleeping. Her golden eyes were open. At a second glance I recognized that fixity of stare—she was engaged in intense mind-seek, and I did not disturb her. Whatever she so listened to was of absorbing interest.

As I was backing out, not wanting to trouble her, the rigid tension broke. Her head lifted a little. But I waited for her to communicate first.

"There is one who comes, but not he whom you expect."

For I thought of the high priest coming for the receipt.

"He is not of the same mind as those who hired our aid," she continued. "Rather is he of an opposite will—"

"A rebel?"

"No. This one wears the same robe as the other temple men. But he does not share their wishes. He thinks it ill done, close to evil, to take these treasures from the sanctuary he serves. He believes that in retaliation his god will bring down ill upon all who aid in such a crime, for such it is to him. He is not one who tempers belief because of a change in the winds of fortune. Now he comes, because he deems it his duty, to deliver the curse of his god. For he serves a being who knows more of wrath than of love and justice. He comes to curse us—"

"To curse only—or to fight?" I asked.

"Do not think of the one as less than the other! In some ways a curse can be a greater weapon, when it is delivered by a believer."

To say that I would scoff at that is wrong. Any far rover of the sky trails can tell you that there is nothing so strange that it cannot happen on one world or another. I have known curses to slay—but only on one condition, that he who is so cursed is also a believer. Perhaps the priests who had sent their treasure into our holds might so be cursed, believe, and die. But for us of the *Lydis* it was a different matter. We are not men of no belief. Each man has his own god or supreme power. Maelen herself had him she called Molaster, by whom and for whom she fashioned her way of life. But that we might be touched by some god of Thoth I could not accept.

"Accept or not"—she had easily followed my thought—"believe or not, yet a curse, any curse, is a heavy load to carry. For evil begets evil and dark clings to shadows. The curse of a believer has its own power. This man is sincere in what he believes and he has powers of his own. Belief *is* power!"

"You cry a warning?" I was more serious now, for such from Maelen was not to be taken lightly.

"I do not know. Were I what I once was—" Her thoughts were suddenly closed to me. Never had I heard her regret what she had left behind on Yiktor when her own body had taken fatal hurt and her people, in addition, had set upon her the penance of perhaps years in the form she now wore. If she had any times of longing or depression, she held them locked within her. And now this broken sentence expressed a desire to hold again what she had had as a Moon Singer of the Thassa, as a man would reach wistfully for a weapon he had lost.

I knew that her message must be passed on to the captain as soon as possible and I went up to the control cabin. Foss sat watching the visa-plate, which at present showed the line of empty trucks on their way back to Kartum. The snouted weapon still sat just outside the gate, its crew alert about it as if they expected more trouble.

"Hatch closed, cargo sealed," I reported. Though that was only a matter of form. Lidj was in the astrogator's seat, slumped a little in the webbing, as he chewed thoughtfully on a stick of restorative slo-go.

"Maelen says—" I began, not even sure if I had their full attention. But I continued with the report.

"Cursing now," Foss commented as I finished. "But why? We are supposed to be saving their treasures for them, aren't we?"

"Schism in the temple, yet," Lidj said in answer to the captain's first question. "It would seem that this High Priest has more than one complication to make life interesting for him. It is rather to be wondered at why this was not mentioned before we accepted contract." His jaws clamped shut on the stick.

The visa-plate pictured new action for us. Though the trucks had gone through the gates, the guards there made no move to fall back. However, there was a stir at that barrier. Not more of the army, rather a procession which might have been honoring some feast day of the god.

We could see plainly the dull purple of priestly robes, brightened by dashes of vivid crimson or angry bursts of orange-yellow, as if flames sprouted here and there. We could not hear, but we could see the large drums borne by men on the outer edges of that line of march, drums being vigorously beaten.

"We have that on board which might be as fire to a fuse," Lidj remarked, still watching the screen, chewing at his slo-go. "The Throne of Qur."

I stared at him. One hears of legends. They are the
foundation for much careless talk and speculation. But to
see—actually to lay hands on the fabric of one, that is another matter altogether. That last, the largest crate we had
hoisted aboard—the Throne of Qur!

Who had been the first, the real owners of the treasures
of Thoth? No one could set name to them now. Oddly
enough, though the remains found were obviously products
of a very high civilization, there had never been discovered
any form of writing or record. We had no names for the
kings, queens, nobles, priests, who had left their possessions
so. Thus the finders, of necessity, had given the names of
their own to the finds.

The Throne had been discovered all alone, walled away
in a section by itself at the end of a blind passage in one of
the early-located caches. The adventurer who had bossed
the crew uncovering it had been not a native of Thoth, but
an archaeologist (or so he claimed) from Phaphor. He had
named his discovery for a deity of his home world. Not that
that had brought him luck, perhaps the contrary. For such
christening had offended the priests. The adventurer had
died, suddenly, and the Throne had been speedily claimed
by the temple, in spite of the fact that the priesthood had
earlier sold excavation rights. For that find had been made
in the days before the complete monopoly of the priesthood
had been enforced. To uncover the Throne he had given
his life, as he must have known, for he had made a vain
attempt to reseal that side passage, perhaps hoping to smug-
gle the Throne away. Only it was far too late for that as
soon as it was found.

The Throne had been fashioned for one of a race who

had physically resembled us. The seat was wrought of a red metal, surprisingly light in weight for its durability. Guarding this were two side pieces, the tops of which furnished arms, and those reared as the heads of unknown creatures, all overlaid with scales of gold and burnished green, with eyes of milky white stones. But it was the flaring, towering back which was its chief marvel. For it seemed to be a wide spread of feathers so delicately fashioned of gold and green that they might once have been real fronds. And the tip of each feather was widened to enclose a blue-green gem, a full one hundred of them in all by count.

But the real peculiarity of the piece, apart from the skill and wonderful craftsmanship, was that those blue-green stones and the milky ones set in the arms were, as far as anyone had been able to discover, not only not native to Thoth but unknown anywhere else. Nor were their like set into any other object so far found on this planet.

Once revealed, the Throne had been moved to the temple in Kartum, where it formed one of the main attractions. Since a close inspection was allowed only after endless waiting and under strict supervision, not much had since been learned of it—though images of it appeared on every tape dealing with Thoth.

The procession by the gate moved out toward the *Lydis*. And those bright red and yellow touches were now seen as wide scarves or shawls resting about the shoulders of the center core of marchers, strung out behind a single man. He was tall, standing well above those immediately about him, and so gaunt that the bones of his face were almost death's-head sharp. There was no softness in that face, nothing but deeply graven lines which spelled fanaticism. His mouth moved as though he were speaking, shouting, or chanting along with the drums which flanked him. His eyes were fastened on the *Lydis*.

I was aware of movement beside me—Maelen was there, her head strained at an angle to watch the screen. I stooped and picked her up that she might see more easily. Her body was more solid, heavier, than it appeared.

"A man of peril, a strong believer," she told me. "Though he is not like our Old Ones—yet he could be, were he properly schooled in the Way of Molaster. Save that such as he have not the open heart and mind that are needful. He sees but one path and is prepared to give all, even life, to achieve what he wishes. Such men are dangerous—"

Lidj glanced over his shoulder. "You are right, little one." He must have picked up her full mind-send. To my shipmates Maelen was all glassia, of course. Only Griss Sharvan had ever seen her in her Thassa body, and even he now seemed unable to connect animal with woman. They knew she was not in truth as she seemed, but they could not hold that ever in mind.

The procession of priests formed a wedge, with their leader at its tip—a spear point aimed at the ship. We still could not hear, but we saw the drummers rest their sticks. Yet the lips of the tall priest still moved and now also his hands. For he stooped and caught up a handful of the trampled, sandy soil. This he spat upon, though he looked not at it, but ever to the ship.

Having spat, he rolled it back and forth between his palms. And now and then he raised it higher, seemed to breathe into what he rolled and kneaded so.

"He curses," Maelen reported. "He calls upon his god to

curse that which would take from Thoth the treasures of
the temple, and all those who aid in the matter. And he
swears that the treasure shall be returned, though those who
take it will then be dead and blasted—and for its return he
shall wait where he now stands."

The priest's lips no longer moved. Two of his followers
pushed forward, one on either side. They whipped from
beneath their cloaks two lengths of matting, and these they
spread upon the ground one over the other. When they had
done, though he never looked once at them but only to the
Lydis, the priest knelt upon that carpet, his hands crossed
upon his breast. Nor did he afterward stir, while his followers, drums and all, withdrew some paces.

Now from the gate came a small surface car which de-
toured around the kneeling priest in a very wide swing.
And it approached the *Lydis*.

"Our take-off authorization." Lidj climbed from his seat.
"I'll go get it—the sooner we lift the better."

He put the uneaten portion of his slo-go back into its
covering, stowed it in a seam pocket, and started from the
cabin. With take-off sure to follow soon, we all scattered,
making for our posts, ready to strap down. Maelen I aided
into her upper berth, laced the protective webbing which
she could not manage with her paws, then dropped into my
own place. As I lay waiting for the signal I thought of the
kneeling priest.

Unless we did make a second trip to pick up more cargo,
he was going to have a long wait. And what if we did return, having made our first delivery to Ptah? Would such
a return prove him so wrong that he would not only lose
his followers but be shaken in his own belief?

"Let us return first—" Maelen's thought came.

There is no betraying intonation in thoughts as there sometimes is in voices. Yet there was something— Did she really believe some ill luck would come to us?

"The Scales of Molaster hang true and steady for those of good will. Any evil in this matter is not of our doing. Yet I do not like—"

The signal for blast-off cut across that. She shut her mind as one might shut his mouth. We lay waiting for the familiar discomfort as the *Lydis* headed up and out—not to the stars this time, but to the fourth planet of the system, a pale crescent now showing in the western sky.

Since we did not go into hyper for such a short trip, we unstrapped as soon as we were on stable speed. Also we were now in free fall, a condition which is never comfortable—though we had been accustomed to it practically from birth. Maelen did not like it at all and preferred to spend such periods in her take-off webbing. I saw that she was as comfortable as might be under the circumstances and then pulled my way along to Lidj's quarters.

But I found, to my amazement, that my superior was not alone. Though he had discarded the robe and cape of his calling, the shaven head of the man lying on the cargo-master's own bunk was plainly that of a priest. We had not been prepared for any passenger; at least I had not been informed of one. And it was so seldom that a Free Trader carried any but a member of the crew that I looked quickly to Lidj for enlightenment. The priest himself lay limp, held by take-off webbing still, appearing totally unconscious.

Lidj waved me outside the cabin and followed. He pulled shut the sliding panel to seal the cabin.

"A passenger—"

"He had orders we had to accept," Lidj informed me. I could see he had little liking for the matter. "He not only brought a warning, to rise as soon as we could, but authorization from the high priest for him to see our cargo to its destination and take charge there. I do not know what pot has boiled over down there—but our Thothian charterers wanted us away as fast as rockets could raise us. At least we can do with one extra aboard, as long as he is going no farther than Ptah."

Chapter 3

MAELEN

I lay in my assigned resting place in this ship and fought once again my weary battle, that battle which I could never share with another, not even with this outlander who had fought a like one in his time. I who was once Maelen, Moon Singer, and (as I know now) far too arrogant in my pride of deed and word, believing that I alone had an accounting with fate and that all would go according to my desire.

Well do we of the Thassa need to remember the Scales of Molaster, wherein the deeds of our bodies, the thoughts of our minds, the wishes of our hearts, will be weighed against truth and right!

Because I had been so weighed and found wanting, now I went in other guise, that of my small comrade Vors. And Vors had willingly given me her body when my own had failed me. So I must not belittle or waste the great sacrifice she had made. Thus I willed myself to endure and endure and endure—to fight this battle not once but again and again, and again and again.

I had chosen, as a Moon Singer who must learn to be one
with other living things, to run the high places of Yiktor in
animal guise, and had so fulfilled my duty. Yet that had
been always with the comfortable knowledge that my own
body waited for my return, that this exile was only for a
time. While now—

Always, though, I was still Maelen—myself—ME; yet
also there was an occupying part which still held the essence of Vors. Much as I had loved and honored her for the
great thing she had done for me, yet also I must struggle
against the instincts of this body, to remain as much as I
could only a temporary indweller. And always was the
brooding shadow of a new fear—that there would be no
escape ever, that through the years Vors would become
more and more, Maelen less and less.

I longed to ask my companion—this alien Krip Vorlund
—whether such a fear had ridden him when he had run as
a barsk. Yet I could not admit to any that I carried such
unease in me. Though whether that silence was born of
some of my old pride and need to be mistress of the situation, or whether it was a curb which was needful, I did not
know. It remained that I must play my role as best I could.
But also I welcomed those times when it was given me to
play some necessary part in the life of the *Lydis*, for then it
seemed that Maelen was wholly in command again. So it
had been that during those last hours on Thoth I had been
able to forget myself and enter into the venture of the ship.

Yet I lay now and my thoughts were dark, for I remembered the priest who had ceremoniously cursed us. As I had
told Krip, there is power in the pure belief of such a man.
Though he had used no wand or staff to point us out to the

Strengths of the Deep Dark, still he had called upon what
he knew to encompass us. And—I had not been able to
reach his mind; there had been a barrier locking me out as
securely as if he had been an Old One.

Now I lay on the bunk, held snug by the webbing (for
with all my shipboard life I have never been able to adjust
well to free fall)—I lay there and used mind-seek.

Those of the *Lydis* were as always. I touched only lightly
the surface of their thoughts. For to probe, unless that is
desperately needed, is a violation to which no living being
should subject another. But in my seeking I came upon another mind and—

I swung my head around, reached with my teeth for the
lacing which held me. Then sane reason took control, and
I sent a call to Krip. His reply was instant—he must have
read my concern.

"What is it?"

"There is one on board from Thoth. He means us ill!"

There was a pause and then his answer came clearly.

"I have him under my eyes now. He is unconscious; he
has been so since the ship lifted."

"His mind is awake—and busy! Krip, this man, he is
more than all others we met on Thoth. He is akin, closely
akin, to the one who cursed us. Watch him—watch him
well!"

But even then I did not realize how different he was,
this stranger, nor just how much we had to fear him. For,
as with him who had cursed us, there was a barrier behind
which he hid more than half his thoughts. And though I
could not read them, I did sense peril there.

"Do not doubt, he shall be watched."

It was as if the stranger had heard what had passed between us. Perhaps he did. For there followed a swift sub-
duing of the emanations of his mind. Though that could
have come from a bodily weakness also. But I was on guard,
as if in truth I walked a sentry's beat in the belly of the
Lydis.

There is no night or day, morn or evening, in a ship.
Which was something I had found hard to adjust to when
first I came on board. Just as the narrow spaces of the cab-
ins, the corridors, were prison-like for one who never had
any home save the wagons of the Thassa, had always lived
by choice beyond man-made walls. There was always an
acrid scent here. And sometimes the throbbing of the engines which powered us from star to star seemed almost
more than I could bear, so that my only escape was into
the past and my memories. No night or day, save those
which the Traders arbitrarily set for themselves, divided
into orderly periods of sleep and waking.

Once the ship was in flight and set on course, there was
little which had to be done to keep her so. Krip had early
shown me that her crew did not lack occupation, however.
Some of them created with their hands, making small things
which amused them, or which they could add to their trade
goods. Others busied their minds, learning from their store
of information tapes. So did they labor to keep the ship
from becoming their prison also.

For Krip—well, perhaps it was for him now as it was for
me, and the body he wore influenced him a little. Because
he was outwardly Thassa, he asked of me my memories,
wanting to learn all he could of my people. And I shared
with him freely, save for such things which could not be

spread before any outlander. So we both escaped into a world beyond the throbbing cabin walls.

Now a little later he returned, ready for the sleep period. Was there any change in what I had learned about our passenger, he asked. Lidj had taken it upon himself, after my warning, to give the man a certain drug which was meant to ease lift-off and which should keep him in slumber for much of our voyage.

No, no change, I answered. And so accustomed had I become to the ship's pattern that, I, too, felt the need of sleep.

I was sharply awakened from my rest, as sharply as if a noose of filan cord had closed about my body, jerking me upright. I found myself in truth fighting the webbing which held me fast to the bunk, even as my mind steadied.

For a dazed moment or two, I could not guess what had so roused me. Then I knew that I no longer felt the ever-present beat of the engine, but rather there was a break in the smooth rhythm. And only a second later a shrill sound came from above my head, issuing from the intercom system of the ship—a warning that all was not well with the *Lydis*.

Krip rolled out of the lower bunk. Since we were in free fall his too-swift movement carried him against the other wall with bruising force. I heard him give a muttered exclamation as he caught at a wall rack and clawed his way back to where I lay. Holding on with one hand, he ripped loose my webbing.

Now that the first warning had awakened us, words came from the intercom, booming like a signal of doom.

"All off-duty personnel, strap down for orbiting!"

Krip paused, his hand still on my webbing, while I clung
with my great claws to the bunk so I would not float away,
unable to govern my going. Then he responded to orders,
pushing me back, making me secure again before he returned to his own place.

"We cannot have reached Ptah!" I was still shaken from
that sudden awakening.

"No—but the ship—"

He did not need to continue. Even I, who was no real
star voyager, could feel the difference. There was a catch
in the rhythm of the engines.

I dared not use mind-touch, lest I disturb some brain
needed to concentrate on the ship's well-being. But I tried
mind-seek. Perhaps it was instinct which aimed that first
at the stranger in our midst.

I have no idea whether I cried out aloud. But instantly
Krip answered me. And when he read my discovery his
alarm was near fear.

I am—was—a Moon Singer. As such, I used the wand.
I could beam-read. I have wrought the transfer of bodies
under the three rings of Sotrath. By the grace of Molaster
I have done much with my talent. But this that I now
touched upon was new, alien, dark, and destructive beyond
all my reckoning.

For there flowed from that priest as he lay a current of
pure power. And I could slip along it, as I did, drawing
Krip's thought with me, through the *Lydis*, down to something that lay below those engines which were her life—
something in the cargo hold.

And that mind power released the force of what lay in

hiding, which had been cunningly attuned to the thought of one man alone. So that there now emanated from that hidden packet a more powerful force than any thought, and a deadly one, acting upon the heart of the *Lydis* to slow the beat of her engines, make them sluggish. And in time it would bring about their failure.

I tried to dam that compelling force flowing from the mind of the priest. But it was as if the current of energy were encased in the Rock of Tormora. It could be neither cut nor swayed from its purpose. Yet I sensed that if it might be halted, then the packet would fail in turn. Learning that, Krip sent his own message:

"The man then, if not his thought—get to the man!"

Straightway I saw he was right. Now I ceased my fight against that current and joined with Krip to seek out Lidj, who should be nearest to the stranger. And so we warned the cargomaster, urging physical action on his part.

It came! That current of feeding energy pulsed, lessened, surged again—then sparked weakly and was gone. The vibration in the ship steadied for perhaps four heartbeats. Then it, too, flickered off. I could feel through the *Lydis* the surge of will of those in her, their fear and need to hold that engine steady.

Then came the return of gravity. We were in orbit—but where and—

My glassia body was not fashioned to take such strains. Though I fought frantically to retain consciousness, I failed.

There was a flat-sweet taste in my mouth; moisture trickled from my muzzle. That part of me which was Vors remembered blood. I ached painfully. When I forced open my eyes I could see only through a mist. But the roof of the cabin was steadily up and I was pulled to the bunk by a gravity greater than that of Thoth.

We had set down. Were we back on Thoth? I doubted it. Hooking my claws against the sides of the bunk, I was able in spite of the webbing to wriggle closer to the edge, look down to see how it had fared with my cabinmate.

As he pushed himself up his eyes met mine. There was a sudden look of concern—

"Maelen!" he said aloud. "You are hurt!"

I turned attention to my body. There were bruises, yes. And blood had issued from my nose and mouth to bedaub my fur. Yet all hurts were small, and I reported it so.

Thus we planeted, not on Thoth, nor on Ptah, which had been our goal, but on Sekhmet. Strange names, all these. Krip had long since told me that the early space explorers of his race were wont to give to suns and their attendant worlds the names of gods and goddesses known to the more primitive peoples of their own historic past. And where those worlds had no native inhabitants to use a rival name, those of the Terran explorers were accepted.

These of the system of Amen-Re were so named from legend. And Krip had shown me the symbols on the map edge to identify each. They had come from the very far past. Set, too fiery to support life, had the picture of a saurian creature; Thoth, that of a long-beaked bird. Ptah was human enough, but Sekhmet was represented in that company by the furred head of a creature which Krip knew and had seen in his own lifetime and which he called a "cat."

These cats had taken to space voyaging easily and had

been common on ships in the early days—though now they were few. Only a small number were carefully nurtured in the asteroid bases of the Traders. A cat's head had Sekhmet, but the body of a woman. What powers the goddess had represented, Krip did not know. Such lore was forgotten. But this world she had given her name to was not of good repute.

It had heavier gravity than Thoth or Ptah, and was so forbidding that, though there had been attempts to colonize it, those had been given up. A few prospectors came now and then, but they had discovered nothing which was not present also on Ptah and much more easily obtained there. Somewhere on its land mass was a Patrol beacon for the relaying of messages. But for the rest it was left to its scouring winds, its lowering skies, and what strange life was native to it.

Not only had we set down on this bleak world—which act was a feat of skill on the parts of our pilot and engineer —but we were in a manner now prisoners here. For that energy which had played upon our engines had done such damage as could not be repaired without supplies and tools which the *Lydis* did not carry.

As for the priest, we had no answers out of him, for he was dead. Lidj, aroused by our warning, had struck quickly. His blow, meant to knock the Thothian unconscious, had not done the harm; rather it was as if the sudden cessation of the act of sabotage had recoiled, burning life out of him. So we did not know the reason for the attack, save that it must have been aimed at keeping us from Ptah.

What was left to us now was to make secure our own safety. Somewhere hidden among these roughly splintered hills (for this land was all sharp peaks and valleys so deep and narrow that they might have been cut into the planet by the sword of an angry giant) there was a Patrol beacon. To reach that and broadcast for help was our only hope.

Within the shell of the *Lydis* was a small two-man flitter, meant to be used for exploration. This was brought out, assembled for service. Over the broken terrain such a trip in search of a beacon which might lie half the world away was a chancy undertaking. And though all the crew were ready to volunteer, it was decided that they should draw lots for the search party.

This they did, each man drawing from a bowl into which they had dropped small cubes bearing their rank symbols. And chance so marked down our astrogator Manus Hunold and second engineer Griss Sharvan.

They took from the stores, making packs of emergency rations and other needs. And the flitter was checked and rechecked, taken up on two trial flights, before Captain Foss was assured it would do.

I had said that this was a planet of evil omen. Though I found nothing by mind-seek to indicate any menace beyond that of the very rugged nature of the surface and the darkness of the landscape. Dark that landscape was.

There are many barren stretches of waste on Yiktor. The high hill country, which is the closest thing to home territory the Thassa now hold, is largely what the lowland men term desert waste. Yet there is always a feeling of light, of freedom, therein.

But here the overpowering atmosphere was one of darkness. The rocky walls of the towering escarpments were of a black or very dark-gray stone. What scanty vegetation there was had a ghostly wanness, being of a pallid gray hue. Or else it nearly matched the rocks in whose crevices it grew, dusky nodules so unpleasant to look upon that to touch them would require a great effort of will.

Even the sand which rose in dunes across this open space where Captain Foss had brought us in for a masterly landing was more like the ashes of long-dead fires—so powdery and fine (save where our deter rockets had fused it) that it held no footprint. Clouds of it were whirled into the air by the cold winds—winds which wailed and cried as they cut through the tortured rock of the heights. It was a land which was an enemy to our kind and which made plain that hostility as the hours passed.

It was those winds which were the greatest source of concern for the flitter. If such gusts grew stronger, the light craft could not battle a passage over dangerously rough country.

Some rewiring and careful work on the com of the *Lydis* had brought a very weak suggestion of a signal. So our comtech Sanson Korde was certain that there was a beacon somewhere on the land where we had set down. A very small piece of doubtful good fortune.

For me there was little enough to do. My paws were not designed to work on the flitter. So I set myself another task, prowling around among those grim rocks, listening with every talent I had—of body and mind—for aught which might live here and mean us ill.

Sekhmet was not devoid of animal life. There were small scuttling insects, things which hid in the breaks between stones. But none of them thought, as we measure mind power. Of larger creatures I discovered not a trace. Which

did not mean that such could not exist somewhere, just
that if they did they were beyond the range of my present
search.

Though I picked up no spark of intelligent life, there was
something else here which I could not explain—a sensation
of a hovering just beyond my range of conscious search. It
was a feeling I had never known before save in one place,
and there I had good reason to expect such. In the highest
lands of Yiktor the Thassa have their own places. Once,
legend tells us, we were a settled people even as the low-
landers are today. We knew the confinement of cities, the
rise of permanent walls ever about us.

Then there came a time when we made a choice which
would change not only those alive to make it then, but the
generations born to follow them—to turn aside from works
made by hands to other powers, invisible, immeasurable.
And it was the choice of those faced by such a splitting of
the life road to take that which favored mind over body.
So gradually it was less and less needful for us to be rooted
in one place. Possessions had little meaning. If a man or
woman had more than he needed he shared with the less
fortunate.

We became rovers, more at home in the lands of the
wilds than those which had held our forefathers rooted. But
still there were certain sacred sites which were very old, so
old that their original use had long since vanished even
from the ancient tales. And these we resorted to on occa-
sions when there was a need that we gather for a centering
of the power—for the raising up of an Old One, or a like
happening.

These sites have an atmosphere, an aura, which is theirs

alone. So that they come alive while we abide there, welcoming us with a warmth of spirit as restoring as a draft of
clear water is to a man who has long thirsted. And this feeling—of vast antiquity and purpose—was something I well
knew.

But here— Why did I have something of the same sensation—of an old, old thing with a kernel of meaning, a
meaning I did not understand? It was as if I had been presented with a record roll which must be learned, yet the
symbols on it were so alien they sparked no meaning in my
mind. And this feeling haunted me whenever I made the
rounds of our improvised landing field. Yet never could I
center it in any one direction so that I might explore further and discover the reason of its troubling. I felt it only
as if it were part of the dry, grit-laden air, the bitter wind
wailing in the rocks.

I was not the only troubled one, but that which occupied
the minds of my companions was a different matter. That
the priest had triggered the device which had brought
about our disaster they knew. The device itself had been
found, and in a surprising place. For a careful search had
led them to the Throne of Qur. First they thought that
what they sought would be within the crate which covered
that. But that was not so. They fully exposed the Throne
and discovered nothing. Then they began a careful search,
inch by inch, of the piece itself, using their best detector.
Thus Lidj had uncovered a cavity in the towering back.
Pressure upon two of the gems there had released a spring.
Within was a box of dull metal.

The radiation reading was such that he put on protective
gloves before he forced it out of its tight setting, transferring

it into a shielded holder which was then taken out of the
ship to be put among the rocks where whatever energy it
broadcast could do no harm. These Traders had traveled
far and had a wide knowledge of many worlds; yet the
workmanship of that box and the nature of the energy it
employed were unknown to them.

Save that they agreed on one thing, that it was not of
Thothian making, since it was manifest that the technology
there was too primitive to produce such a device.

"Unless," Captain Foss commented, "these priests in
their eternal treasure-seeking have uncovered secrets they
are not as quick to display as the other things they have
found. It is apparent that that hollow in the Throne was
not lately added, but must have been a part of it since its
first fashioning. Was this also left over from that time?
We have a dead man, a secret which is dangerous. We have
a weapon used at just the right point in our voyage to force
us to Sekhmet. And this adds up to a sum I dislike."

"But why— We could have been left derelict in space—"
Shallard, the engineer, burst out. "It was only by the favor
of fortune we were able to make a good landing here."

Foss stared across the rocks and the shifting dunes of
powdery sand.

"I wonder—on that I wonder," he said slowly. And then
he turned to the two who had drawn the lots for the beacon
search. "I am beginning to believe that the sooner we contact authority the better. Prepare to take off in the next lull
of the wind."

Chapter 4

MAELEN

So did they wing off in the flitter. In that was a device which kept them in contact with the *Lydis*, though they did not report more than passing above the same landscape as we saw. However, Foss kept in contact with them by the com unit of the ship, and his unease was as clear as if he shouted his thoughts aloud.

That we had been sabotaged it was unnecessary to question. But the reason remained unclear. Had we been delayed before take-off on Thoth, that would have been simple. Either the rebel forces or that fanatical priest could have done so. Only this stroke had come in mid-flight.

Had we been meant to land on Sekhmet? The captain was dubious about that—such depended too much on chance. He was more certain the attack had been meant to leave the *Lydis* helpless in space. And the rest of the crew agreed with him. At least on-planet one had more of a fighting chance; we might not have been given even that small advantage. In either case the threat was grave, so that even before he gave his orders to Korde, the com-tech had opened panels, was studying the maze of wiring behind them. There was a chance that these elements could be converted to a super-com, something with which to signal for help if the voyage of the flitter failed. The Traders were well used to improvising when the need arose.

Night was coming—though the day on Sekhmet had been hardly more than pallid dusk, the cloud cover lying so thickly across the riven hills. And with that flow of shadows the cold was greater. So I bushed my fur, not consciously, but by instinct.

Krip summoned me back to the ship, for they planned to seal themselves within, using that as a fort, even as it had been outside Kartum. I made one more scout sweep—found nothing threatening. Nothing which I could point to and say, "This is danger." Yet—

As the hatch closed behind me, the warmth and light of the Lydis giving a sense of security, still I was troubled by that other feeling—that we were ringed about by— What?

I used my claws to climb the ladder which led to the living quarters. But I was opposite the hatch of the hold wherein sat the Throne when I paused, clinging to the rungs. My head swung to that closed door as if drawn by an overwhelming force. So great was the pull that I hunched from the ladder itself to the space by the door, my shoulder brushing its surface.

That box which had wrought our disaster was now safely gone; I had watched its outside disposal. But from this room flowed a sense of—"life" is the closest I could come to describing it. I might now be in the field of some invisible communication. There was not only the mental alert, but a corresponding tingle in my flesh. My fur was rippling as it might under the touch of a strong wind. I must have

given forth a mind-call, for Krip's answer came quickly:
"Maelen! What is it?"

I tried to reply, but there was so little of which I could
make a definite message. Yet what I offered was enough to
summon them to me with speed—Krip, the captain, and
Lidj.

"But the box is gone," Captain Foss said. He stepped to
one side as Lidj crowded past to reopen the sealed hatch.
"Or— Can there be another?"

Krip's hand was on my head, smoothing that oddly ruffled fur. His face expressed his concern, not only for what
danger might lurk here, but in a measure for me also. For
he knew that I could not tell what lay behind the door, and
my very ignorance was an additional source of danger. I
was shaken now as I had never been in the past.

Lidj had the door open. And, with that, light flashed
within. There sat the Throne, facing us squarely. They had
not recrated it as yet. Only the cavity in the back was closed
again. The captain turned to me.

"Well, what is it?"

But in turn I looked to Krip. "Do you feel it?"

He faced the Throne, his face now blank of expression,
his dark Thassa eyes fixed. I saw his tongue pass over his
lower lip.

"I feel—something—" But his puzzlement was strong.

Both the other Traders looked from one of us to the
other. It was plain they did not share what we felt. Krip
took a step forward—put his hand to the seat of the
Throne.

I cried aloud my protest as a glassia growl. But too late.
His finger tips touched the red metal. A visible shudder

shook his body; he reeled back as if he had thrust his hand into open fire—reeled and fell against Lidj, who threw out an arm just in time to keep him from sliding to the floor. The captain rounded on me.

"What is it?" he demanded.

"Force—" I aimed mind-speech at him. "Strong force. I have never met its like before."

He jerked away from the Throne. Lidj, still supporting Krip, did the same.

"But why don't we also feel it?" the Captain asked, now eyeing the Throne as if he expected it to discharge raw energy into his very face.

"I do not know—perhaps because the Thassa are more attuned to what it exudes. But it is broadcasting force, and out there"—I swung my head to indicate the wall of the ship—"there is something which draws such a broadcast."

The captain studied the artifact warily. Then he came to the only decision a man conditioned as a Free Trader could make. The safety of the *Lydis* was above all else.

"We unload—not just the Throne, all this. We cache it until we learn what's behind it all."

I heard Lidj suck in his breath sharply. "To break contract—" he began, citing another part of the Traders' creed.

"No contract holds that a cargo of danger must be transported, the more so when that danger was not made plain at the acceptance of the bargain. The *Lydis* has already been planeted through the agency of this—this treasure! We are only lucky that we are not now in a drifting derelict because of it. This must go out—speedily!"

So, despite the dark, floodlights were strung, and once more the robos were put to work. This time they trundled to the hatches all those crates, boxes, and bales which had been so carefully stowed there on Thoth. Several of the robos were swung to the ground and there set to plowing through the dunes, piling the cargo within such shelter as a ridge of rock afforded. And there last of all was put the Throne of Qur, its glittering beauty uncovered, since they did not wait to crate it again.

"Suppose"—Lidj stood checking off the pieces as the robos brought them along—"this is just what someone wants—that we dump it where it can be easily picked up?"

"We have alarms rigged. Nothing can approach without triggering those. And then we can defend it." The captain spoke to me. "You can guard?"

It was very seldom during the months since I had joined the ship that he had asked any direct service of me, though he acknowledged I had talents which his men did not possess. What I had I gave willingly, before it was asked. It would seem now that he hesitated a little, as if this was a thing for which I ought to be allowed to volunteer.

I answered that I could and would—though I did not want to come too close to that pile of cargo, especially the glittering Throne. So they rigged their alarms. But as they went into the ship again, Krip came down the ramp.

His adventure in the hold had so affected him that he had had to withdraw for a space to his cabin. Now he wore the thermo garments made for cold worlds, the hood pulled over his head, the mittens on his hands. And he carried a weapon I had seldom seen him use—a blaster.

"Where do you think you're—" the captain began when Krip interrupted.

"I stay with Maelen. Perhaps I do not have her power,

but still I am closer to her than the rest of you are. I stay."

At first the captain looked ready to protest, then he nodded. "Well enough."

When they had gone and the ramp was back in the ship, Krip waded through the drifting sand to look at the Throne —though he kept well away from it, I was glad to note.

"What—and why?"

"What and why, indeed," I made answer. "There are perhaps as many answers as I have claws to unsheathe. Perhaps the captain is wrong and we were indeed meant to land here, even to unload the cargo. Only that dead priest could answer us truly what and why."

I sat up on my haunches, balancing awkwardly as one must do in a body fashioned to go on four feet when one would be as erect as one ready to march on two. The wind curled about my ribs and back in a cold lash, yet my fur kept me warm. However, the sand-ash arose in great choking swirls, shifting over the Throne of Qur.

Now I squinted against that blowing grit, my gaze fixed upon the chair. Did—did I see for an instant divorced from true time what my eyes reported? Or did I imagine it only?

Did the dust fashion, even as if it clung to an invisible but solid core, the likeness of a body enthroned as might be a judge to give voice upon our affairs?

It was only for an instant that it seemed so. Then that shadow vanished. The wind-driven dust collapsed into a film on the red metal. And I do not think Krip saw it at all.

There was nothing more in the night. Our lights continued to shine on the air-spun dust, which built small hillocks around the boxes. My most alert senses could not pick up any echo among the rocks or in the near hills. We might have dreamed it all, save that we knew we had not. A fancy that it had been done to force the cargo out into the open settled so deep in my mind that I almost believed it the truth. But if we had been so worked upon to render the treasure vulnerable, no one now made any move to collect it.

Sekhmet had no moon to ride her cloudy sky. Beyond the circle of lights the darkness was complete. Shortly after the ship was sealed again, the wind died, the sand and dust ceased to drift. It was very quiet, almost too much so—for the feeling that we were waiting grew stronger.

Yet there came no attack—if any menace did lurk. However, in the early morning something occurred, in its way a greater blow at the *Lydis*, at our small party, than any attack of a formless evil. For this was concrete, a matter of evidence. The flitter's broadcast suddenly failed. All efforts to re-establish contact proved futile. Somewhere out in the waste of hills, mountains, knife-sharp valleys, the craft and her crew of two must be in trouble.

Since the *Lydis* carried only one flitter, there was no hope of manning a rescue flyer. Any such trip must be done overland. And the terrain was such as to render that well-nigh impossible. We could depend now only on the improvised com in the ship. To gather volume enough to signal off-world, Korde must tap our engines. Also, for any such broadcast there would be a frustrating time lag.

As was customary among the Traders, the remaining members of the crew assembled to discuss the grim future, to come to an agreement as to what must be done. Because Free Traders are bound to their ships, owning no home world of earth and stone, water and air, they are more

closely knit together than many clans. That they could
abandon two of their number lost in the unknown was unthinkable. Yet to search on foot for them was a task defeated before begun. Thus caught between two needs, they
were men entrapped. Shallard agreed that the *Lydis* might
just be able to rise from her present site. But that she could
again make a safe landing he doubted. All his delving into
the engines did not make plain just what had hit her power,
but important circuits were burned out.

Again, as was the custom, each man offered what sug-
gestions he could. Though in the end there was only one
which could be followed—that the off-world com must be
put into operation. It was then that Lidj voiced a warning
of his own.

"It cannot be overlooked," he told them, "that we may
have been pulled into a trap. Oh, I know that it is just on
the edge of possibility that we were meant to fin down here
on Sekhmet. On the other hand, how many cases of actual
looting of ships in space are known? Such tales are more
readily found on the fiction tapes, where the authors are
not bound by the technical difficulties of such a maneuver.
I think we can assume that the cargo is what led to sabotage. All right—who wants it? The rebels, that fanatic of a
priest? Or some unknown party, who hopes to gather in
loot worth more stellars than we could count in a year—if
they could lift it from us and transport it out?

"Once away from this system, it would be a matter of
possession being nine-tenths of the law. Only here are the
claims of the priesthood recognized as legal. You have heard
of the Abna expedition, and the one that Harre Largo managed ten years back? They got in, found their treasure, got

out again. The priests yelled themselves near black in the face over both, but the finds were legitimate, made by the men who ran the stuff out—they were not stolen.

"Then there are the laws of salvage. Think about those carefully. Suppose the *Lydis* had crashed here. That would cancel our own contract. Such an accident would open up a neat loophole which would be easy to use. Anyone finding a wrecked ship on an unsettled world—"

"That would only apply," cut in Captain Foss, "if all the crew were dead."

He did not have to underline that for us. A moment later he added: "I think we can be sure this is sabotage. And certainly this idea of a third party is logical. It could explain what happened to the flitter."

As he said, it all fitted together neatly. Yet, perhaps because my way of thinking was Thassa and not Trader, because I depended not upon machines and their patterns, I could not wholly accept such an explanation. There was something in what I had felt by the Throne of Qur, in that lowering feeling of being watched, which did not spring from any ordinary experience. No, in an indefinable way it was oddly akin to the Thassa. And I was sure that this affair was of a different nature from those of the Traders.

But because I had no proof, nothing but this feeling, I did not offer my suggestion. Those on the *Lydis* believed now that they were under siege, must wait for the unknown enemy to show his hand in some manner. And they voted to turn all their efforts to the broadcast for aid.

However, only two of them could provide the knowledgeable assistance Korde needed. For the others, Captain Foss had another task. That cargo now piled in open sight was, he decided, to be hidden as quickly as possible. Once more he disembarked the working robos, while Krip and I went out from the immediate vicinity of the ship in search of a good cache site.

There were plenty of possibilities in this very rough country. But we wanted one which would fulfill the captain's needs best—that being a site which could be sealed once the treasure was stowed. So we examined any narrow crevice, surveyed carefully any promising hole which might give entrance to a cave or other opening.

I was no longer aware of any current flowing between the Throne and some place beyond the valley. In the morning's early light that artifact, now shrouded in dust which clouded its brilliance, was only an inanimate object. One might well believe that imagination had supplied the happenings of the night before, except that it had not. Had that emanation been a kind of beacon, informing others of our position?

If so, once they were sure, they could well have turned off that which made a magnet of the cargo. So, as we went, I mind-searched as well as I could, even though to beam-read properly and at a goodly distance I did not have what I needed most, my lost wand of power, plus the chance for complete concentration—shutting all else out of my mind.

We came at last to a ridge taller than those immediately around our landing site. And the light was brighter, the sullen clouds less heavy. Along the wall—

Some trick of the light, together with a filmy deposit of sand which clung in curve and cut and hollow— I rose to my haunches, straining back my short neck, longing for a better range of vision.

Because the dust and the light made clear something of those lines on the stone. I saw there a design, far too regular in pattern for me to believe that it had been formed by erosion alone, the scouring of the wind-driven sand.

"Krip!"

At my summons he turned back from where he had gone farther down that cut.

"The wall—" I drew his attention to what seemed clearer and clearer the longer I studied it—that pattern so worn by the years that at first it could hardly be distinguished at all.

"What about the wall?" He looked at it. But there was only open puzzlement on his face.

"The pattern there." By now it was so plain to me I could not understand why he also did not see it. "Look—" I became impatient as I pointed as best I could with a forepaw, unsheathing claws as if I could reach up and trace the lines themselves. "Thus—and thus—and thus—" I followed the lines so, in and out. There were gaps, of course, but the over-all spread was firm enough not to need all the parts long weathered away.

He squinted, his eyes obediently following my gestures. Then I saw the dawn of excitement on his face.

"Yes!" His own mittened hand swung up as he, too, traced the design. "It is too regular to be natural. But—" Now I sensed a whisper of alarm in his mind—as if something in the design was wrong.

It was when I looked again, not at the part closer to me, but moving back even farther to catch the whole of it, that I saw it was not the abstract design my eyes had first reported. What was really pictured on the cliffside was a face

—or rather a mask. And that was of something neither human nor of any creature I knew.

But into Krip's mind flashed one word—"CAT!"

Once he had so identified it I could indeed trace a resemblance between it and the small symbol on the old map of the Amen-Re system. Yet it was also different. That head had been more rounded, far closer to a picture one could associate with a living animal. This was a distinctly triangular presentation with the narrowest angle pointing to the foot of the cliff.

In the area at the wider top there were two deep gashes set aslant to form eyes. Deep and very dark, giving one the disturbing impression that they pitted a skull. There was an indication of a muzzle with a lower opening, as if the creature had its mouth half open, while a series of lines made upstanding ears. There was nothing normal about the mask. Yet once it was called to my attention, I could see that it had evolved from a cat's head.

I had felt nothing but interest when I had seen the cat on the chart, a desire to see one of these animals for myself. But this thing—it was not of the same type at all.

The hollow which was the mouth held my interest now. And I went to explore it. Though the opening was so narrow that anyone of human bulk must crouch low to enter, I could do it with ease. In I padded, needing to know the why and wherefore, for so much effort had been expended in making the carving that I was sure it had a purpose.

The space was shallow—hardly more than half again the length of my glassia body. I raised one of my paws and felt before me, for it was too dark here to see. Thus I touched a

surface which was smooth. Yet my seeking claws caught
and ran along grooves, which I traced until I was sure that
those marked divisions of blocks which had been carefully
fitted into place.

When I reported this to Krip I was already sure of what
we might have discovered by chance. While Sekhmet had
never been known to house any treasure (perhaps it had
never been well searched), we could have discovered such
a hiding place. Though we had little time to prove or dis-
prove it.

I tried to work my claw tips between the stones, to see if
they could be so loosened. But it was impossible. When I
scrambled out, Krip had his wrist com uncovered, was re-
porting our find. Though the captain showed some interest,
he urged us now to carry out our original task and locate a
place where the cargo could be cached.

"Not around here." Krip's decision matched mine. "If
they—whoever they may be—do come looking, we need
not direct them in turn to that!" He gestured to the cat's
head.

Thus we turned directly away from that, heading to the
northwest. So we came upon a crevice which the light of
Krip's torch told us deepened into a cave. And since we
had found nothing so good closer to our landing site, we
selected that.

So rough was the terrain that the passage of each laden
robo had to be carefully supervised. Foss wanted no cutting or smoothing of the way to the hiding place. It took
us most of the remaining daylight hours to see all into the
crevice. Once the cargo was stowed, rocks were built into

a stopper, well under the overhang of the outer part of the crevice, where they might be overlooked unless someone was searching with extra care.

Then a small flamer, such as is used for ship repairs, was brought in and the rocks fused into a cork which would take a great deal of time and trouble to loosen.

Lidj made a last inspection. "Best we can do. Now—let's see this other find of yours."

We led them to the cliff face. It was difficult now, though they shone working lights on it, to see the lines which had been more distinct in the early morning. I thought perhaps the dust had largely blown away. Lidj at first professed to distinguish nothing. And it was only when he hunched well down and centered a torch into the mouth, located that inner wall of blocks, that he was convinced the find was not some far flight of imagination.

"Well enough," he admitted then. "What this may lead to"—he held the torch closer to the wall—" can be anyone's guess. Certainly nothing we can explore now. But who knows about later?"

However, I knew that beneath his outer calm he was excited. This was such a find as might return to the *Lydis* all the lost profit from this voyage—perhaps even more.

Chapter 5

KRIP VORLUND

"Men who go looking for trouble never have far to walk."
Lidj leaned back in his chair, his hands folded over his middle. He was not gazing at me, but rather at the wall over my head. In another man his tone might have been one of resignation. But Juhel Lidj was not one to be resigned or lacking in enterprise in any situation, or so it had been so far during our association.

"And we have been looking for trouble?" I dared to prod when he did not add to that statement.

"Perhaps we have, Krip, perhaps we have." Still he watched the wall as if somewhere on it were scrawled or taped the answer to our puzzle. "I don't believe in curses—not unless they are my own. But neither do I know that that priest back on Thoth did not know exactly what he was doing. And, to my belief, he was playing some hand of his own. When the news comes that we are missing, then his credit will go up. The efficiency of his communication with their god will be proven."

"Temple politics?" I thought I followed him. "Then you believe that that is at the bottom of it, that we don't have to be worried about being jumped while here?"

Now he did glance at me. "Don't put words in my mouth, Krip Vorlund. Perhaps my suggestion is just another logical deduction. I'm not a theurgist of Manical, to draw lines on my palm with a sacred crayon, pour a spot of purple wine in the middle, and then read the fate of the ship pictured therein. To my mind there is the smell of temple intrigue in this, that is all. The question which is most important is, how do we get out of their trap?"

That brought back what was uppermost in our minds, the disappearance, if not from the sky of Sekhmet, at least from our visa-screen, of the flitter. This was, judging by the terrain immediately about us, a harsh world, and forced down on such, Hunold and Sharvan would be faced by a desperate choice—if they still lived. Would they struggle on, trying to reach the beacon, or were they already attempting to fight their way back to the *Lydis?* Perhaps it all depended upon how far they judged themselves to be from either goal.

The Traders stand by their own. Such is bred in us, as much as the need for space, the impatience and uneasiness which grips us when we have been too long planetside. It was only the knowledge that without any guides, we ourselves might wander fruitlessly and to no useful purpose, which kept us chained to the *Lydis* and not out searching for our lost shipmates.

"Korde can do it, if it can be done. There is a Patrol asteroid station between here and Thoth. If he can beam

a signal strong enough to reach either that or some cruise
ship of theirs, then we're set."

Patrol? Well, the Patrol is necessary. There must be some
law and order even in space. And their men are always under orders to render assistance to any ship in distress. But
it grated on our Free Trader pride to have to call for such
help. We were far too used to our independence. I spun
the case of a report tape between thumb and forefinger,
guessing just how much this galled our captain.

"One thing on the credit side," Lidj continued. "That
find which your furred friend turned up out there. If there
is a treasure cache here, the priests cannot claim it. But we
can."

He was once more staring at the wall. I did not have to
mind-probe to know what occupied his thoughts. Such a
find would not only render the *Lydis* famous, but perhaps
lift us all to the status of contract men, with enough credits
behind us to think of our own ships. Even more so since
the find was made on a planet where exploration was not
restricted, where more than one such could be turned up.

I had been thinking ever since Maelen had drawn my
attention to those cliff-wall carvings. And I had done some
research among my own store of tapes.

A Free Trader's success depends on many things, luck
being well to the fore among those. So luck had been with
us here, good as well as bad. But the firm base of any
Trader's efficiency is knowledge, not specialized as a tech
must have, but wide—ranging from the legends of desert
rovers on one planet to the habits of ocean plants on another. We listened, we kept records, we went with open

minds and very open ears wherever we planeted, or when we exchanged news with others of our kind.

"When Korde is through with this com hookup, do you suppose he could rig something else?" I knew what I wanted, but the technical know-how to make it was beyond my skill.

"Just what, and for what purpose?"

"A periscope drill." The term might not be the right one, but that was the closest I could come to describing what I had read about in the tapes. "They used such, rigged with an impulse scanner, on Sattra II where the Zacathans were prospecting for the Ganqus tombs. With something like that we might be able to get an idea of what *is* back in the cliff. It saves the labor of digging in where there may be nothing worth hunting. As on Jason, where the tombs of the Three-eyes had already been looted—"

"You have information on this?"

"Just what it does, not the mechanics of it." I shook my head. "You'd have to have a tech work it out."

"Maybe we can—if we have the time. Bring me that note tape."

When I returned to my cabin to get that, Maelen raised her head from the cushion of her forepaws, her gold eyes agleam. Though I saw a glassia, yet when her thoughts met mine it was no animal sharing my small quarters. In my mind she was as I first saw her, slender in her gray-and-red garments, the soft fur of her jacket as bright in its red-gold luxuriance as the silver-and-ruby jewel set between the winging lift of her fair silver brows, her hair piled formally high with ruby-headed pins to hold it. And that picture I held closer because somehow, though she had never brought it

into words between us, she found comfort in the knowledge
that I saw her as the Thassa Moon Singer who saved my
life when I was hunted through the hills of Yiktor.

"There is news?"

"Not yet." I pulled down one of the seats which snapped
up to the wall when not in use. "You cannot contact
them?"

But I need not have asked that. Had she been able, we
would have known it. Her gifts, so much the less compared
to what they had once been, were always at our service.

"No. Perhaps they have gone too far—or perhaps I am
too limited now. But it is not altogether concern for those
of our company missing which lies in your mind now."

I clicked one tape cover against the next, hunting that
which had the notation I wanted. "Maelen, is there any
way to thought-see through the cliff—behind the cat
mask?"

She did not answer me at once. She must have been
considering carefully before she did.

"Mind-send must have a definite goal. If I knew of some
spark of life there I could focus upon it. As it is—no. But—
you have thought of some way?" She had been quick to
pick that up from me.

"Something I heard of—a periscope drill. It might just
work here, so we could learn if we have found a treasure
cache or not. Yes, here it is." I snapped the tape into my
reader, ran it along impatiently, seeking the pertinent
section.

She shared my absorption in that rather vague report
which a fellow Trader, who had been chartered to supply
the Zacathan expedition, had furnished me.

"It seems a complicated machine," she commented, not entirely with favor. Her reaction might have arisen from the Thassa distaste for machines and any need to depend upon them. "But if it works, then I can see it in use here. Also, I believe you are correct in your guess that if this is a treasure cache it will not be the only one to be found on Sekhmet.

"Krip, do you remember how once, long ago it now seems, we spoke of treasure and you said that it could be many things on many worlds, but that each man had his own idea of what it was? Then you added that what would be precious to you was a ship of your own, that that was what your people considered true treasure. Suppose this cache, or another, were to yield enough to give you that. What would you do with such a ship—voyage, as does the *Lydis*, seeking profit wherever chance and trade call you?"

She was right in that a ship was the Trader standard of treasure. Though it would take a sum beyond perhaps even the value of the cargo from Thoth to buy a ship for each member of the *Lydis's* crew. And all finds would be shared. But a ship of my own—

Dreams can be dreamed, but to bring them alive calls for logic and planning. I was in training as a cargomaster and, as I well knew and admitted, a long way from being ready to take full responsibility for top rating even in that berth. I was no pilot, engineer, astrogator. What would I truly do if I had credits in my belt tomorrow which would buy me the ship of my daydreaming?

Again she followed my thoughts.

"Do you remember, Krip Vorlund, how you spoke when

I told you *my* fancy—of taking my little people in a ship to the stars? Could such a treasure buy that ship?"

So she still held to *her* dream? Though perhaps it had now even less chance of realization than mine.

"It would have to be a treasure past all reckoning," I told her soberly.

"Agreed. And I have not gone a-voyaging these past months with a closed mind. The Thassa know Yiktor in width and length, but they know not space. I have learned that there are limits of which I was unaware when I claimed to be a Moon Singer of power. We are but a small people among many, many races and species. Yet to recognize that is a good beginning. With your delving machine do you go hunting, Krip—if the time is given you."

"Lidj thinks—" I told her what the cargomaster had said. But before I had finished, her furred head moved from side to side.

"Such a conclusion is logical. But there is this. Since I first took sentry duty here, I know we have been watched."

"What! By whom—from where?"

"It is because I cannot answer just such questions that I have not given a warning. Whatever it is which forces my unease, it lurks beyond the edge of my probe. I can no longer far-beam-read. The Old Ones took much of my power when they reft from me my wand. There only remains enough to warn. What is here only watches; it has yet made no move. But—tell me. Krip—why is it that a cat face is upon the cliff wall?"

Her sudden change of subject startled me. And I could not give her an answer.

"This is what I mean." Her thought-send was impatient. "The cat is an ancient symbol of Sekhmet, for whom this planet is named. That you told me. But—were not this sun and its attendant worlds given their names originally by some Scout of your people who landed here in exploration? Therefore the cat is an off-world symbol.

"Yet here we find it—or a pattern enough like it so that you say 'cat' at once when you trace it—marking something *not* left by settlers of your kind. Why did these unknown and forgotten earlier ones use the cat mask?"

I had not really thought of that before.

"It must be something left by the first settlers. Perhaps they tried to colonize Sekhmet before the other planets."

"I think not. I think this is far too old. How many years has this system been settled? Do you have such a record?"

"I don't know. If they were of the first wave, perhaps a thousand years, a little less."

"Yet I would judge that carving to be twice, maybe thrice that age. To erode stone so deeply takes a long time. At our places on Yiktor that is so. And the rest of the treasures are not of settler making; they were found by the first men to land. Still we have here a cat mask! Who, and how old, were the gods for whom this system was named—this cat-headed Sekhmet?"

"They were Terran and very old even on that world. And Terra took to space a thousand years ago." I shook my head. "Much history has been forgotten in the weight of years. And Terra is halfway across the galaxy from here. When such gods and goddesses were worshiped, her people had no space travel."

"Perhaps your species did not then go forth from their

parent world. But did any visit them there? The races of the Forerunners—how many such civilizations rose and fell?"

"No one knows, not even the Zacathans, who make the study of history their greatest science and art. And nowadays even Terra is half legend. I have never met a spacefarer who has actually been there, or one who can claim clear descent from its people."

"Fable, legend—in the core of such there exists a small kernel of truth. Maybe here—"

The com over my head crackled and Foss sounded a general message.

"Broadcast now possible. We are sending off-world."

Though whether that effort would avail us, who could tell? I took my tape and went back to Lidj, playing the pertinent portion for him and then again for Shallard. The latter did not seem very hopeful that he and Korde could produce any such instrument, but went off again at last to consult his own records.

Waiting can be very wearying. We set up a watch which did not involve either Korde, always on com duty, or Shallard. Maelen and I shared a term. We made only the rounds of the valley in which the *Lydis* had finned down, not venturing beyond its rim, however much we would have liked to explore near the cat mask or prospect about that for other indications that long-ago men, or other intelligent beings, had been there.

We saw no one, heard nothing; nor was Maelen able to pick up any thought waves to suggest that this was more than a deserted stretch of inhospitable land. However, she continued to affirm that there was an influence of some kind hanging about which puzzled and, I think (though this she did not admit), alarmed her.

Maelen had always been much of an enigma to me. At first her alienness had set a barrier between us, a severance which had been strengthened when she had used her power to save my life by the only method possible—making man into beast. Or rather moving that which was truly Krip Vorlund from one body to another. That the man body had died through mischance had not been her fault, hard as my loss had seemed to me at the time. She had given me the use of a barsk's body. And she had brought me to the one I now wore in turn.

Thassa I walked, though Thassa I did not now live. And perhaps that outer shell of Thassa moved me closer in spirit than I had been before to the Moon Singer, Mistress of Little Ones, that I had known. Sometimes I found myself deliberately trying to tap whatever residue of Thassa might linger in my body, so that I could better understand Maelen.

Three guises I had worn in less than one planetary year— man, beast, Thassa. And the thought ever lurked in the depths of my mind that each was a part of me. Maquad, whose body finally became mine, was long dead. As a Thassa undergoing instruction he had taken on beast form, and in that form he had been killed by an ignorant hunter from the lowlands, poaching on forbidden territory. In his humanoid form the beast spirit had gone mad after a space, unable to adjust—so that what remained was a living husk. I had displaced no one when I took that husk.

But the body which had been Maelen's—that had died. And only because Vors, one of her Little Ones, had offered her spirit a dwelling place had she survived. The Old Ones had condemned her to live as Vors for a time they reckoned by a reading of the stars which hung in Yiktor's skies. But when that time had passed—where would she find a new body?

That question troubled me from time to time, though I strove to hide it from her, having a strange feeling that such speculation would be forbidden, or was wrong to mention, until she herself might clear such uncertainty. But she never had. I wanted to know more of the Thassa, but there was a barrier still raised around certain parts of their lives, and that I dared not breach.

Now we stood together in the early morning, having climbed to the cliff top which was part of the valley rim. Maelen faced out, her head pointing in the direction the flitter had taken as it bore off into the unknown. The wind ruffled her fur just as it also curled about my thermo jacket.

"Out there—it abides," came her thought.

"What does?"

"I do not know, save that it lies there waiting, watching —ever. Or—does it dream?"

"Dream?" Her choice of word surprised me. Though I strove with all the esper talent I had to catch that emanation which appeared so clear to Maelen, I had never yet touched it.

"Dream, yes. There are true dreams which can be foreseeing. Surely you know that." Once more she was impatient. "I dreamed—that I know. Yet the manner of my dream I cannot recall—save in small snatches of light, color, or feeling."

"Feeling?" I sought to lead her on.

"Waiting! That is the feeling!" There was triumph as she solved a problem. "I was waiting for something near me, something of such importance my life depended upon it. Waiting!" She held to the last word as if it were part of an important formula.

"But the rest—"

"A place strange and yet not strange—I knew it and yet knew it not. Krip"— her head swung around—"when you ran as Jorth the barsk, did you not fear that in some ways the beast was becoming greater than the man?"

So did I at last learn her fear, as if she had described a vision of terror. I went to one knee and put my arms about that furred body, drawing it close. I had not thought that this fear would be hers, knowing that body change was a part of Thassa life. But perhaps she was no longer guarded by the safe checks they used on Yiktor.

"You think this may be true for you?"

She was very close to me, passive in my hold, yet still her mind held aloof. Perhaps she already regretted even that small reaching for reassurance.

"I do not know, no longer am I sure." Her admission was painful. "I try—*how* I try—to be Maelen. But if I become all Vors—"

"Then shall I remember Maelen for us both!" What I could offer her I did. And it was the truth! Let her slip back into the animal, yet I would make myself continue to see not fur but firm pale flesh, silver hair, dark eyes in a humanoid face, the grace, the pride, and the beauty of the Moon Singer. "And neither shall I let you forget, Maelen. Never shall I let you forget!"

"Yet I think of a failing memory—" If thought could come as a whisper, so did hers sink so low.

My wrist com buzzed, and I stripped back my mitten to listen to the click of code. Fortune was favoring us. Our off-world signal had raised an answer far sooner than our most optimistic hopes had dared suggest. There was a Patrol Scout coming in and we were now recalled to the *Lydis*.

The Scout set down in the night, braking rockets flaring in a valley near our own. Her crew would not try to reach us until morning, but in the meantime we beamed through to them a full report of all that had happened since our lift-off from Thoth. All except one matter—our find of the cat mask on the cliff.

In return the Scout had news of import for us. The rebellion on Thoth had flared high in Kartum, fed by a split within the loyalist party arising from the cursing of our ship. With priest turned against priest, and the solidarity of the ruling caste so broken, the rebels had found it easy to infiltrate and conquer. Those with whom we had had a contract were now dead. The rebels were demanding the return of the treasure. And there was talk that we had meant all the time to space with it as our spoil. We listened to this and then Foss spoke:

"It seems we now have another problem. Perhaps we did better than we knew when we cached the cargo here. Until we can sort out just who takes lawful custody now, let it remain where it is."

"It is contracted still for Ptah," Lidj pointed out. "We only cached it for fear of its possible influence."

"Our contract was given by men now dead. I want to know the situation on Ptah before we go in there—if the rebels have a foothold there too. Dead men don't own anything, unless you count their tombs. If the government is changed, what we have may be legally claimed elsewhere. To be caught on another planet with a cargo of uncertain origin can put a Trader out of business—perhaps permanently. Until we are sure of the present owners, we want to take no chances of being accused, as it seems we already are, of jacking it all ourselves. I am depositing second-copy contract tapes with the Patrol at once. That will cover us for a while. But we'll leave the cache as it is until we hear from the temple on Ptah."

"What about payment?" Lidj asked. "According to contract we were to take our pick *after* we set down on Ptah. We can't collect before delivery. And a dry run, with repairs unpaid for, is a setback we are not able to take now. We dumped cargo at Kartum to take this on."

"Interference claim—at least to cover repairs?" I ventured. "We can prove it was that box and the priest that brought us here. That ought to make a good claim—"

"Well enough," Lidj agreed. "But get to the fine points of stellar law and this can be argued out for years. If we pick up our pay at the end it will be too late to help us. We could be bankrupt or dead by the time the space lawyers got tired of clicking their jaws over it. We need that carriage fee. In fact, we have to have it if we are going to continue lifting ship!

"On the other hand, we dare not be accused of looting either. The best we can do at present is make a formal Claim of Interference, post our tapes, and ask for an investi-

gation on Ptah—to be made by the Patrol. If they reply
that everything is as usual there, are you willing to chance
delivery?"

We agreed. I wondered a little at Foss's seeming reluc-
tance to proceed without a solemn, signed crew agreement.
Traders are always cautious, to a point. But Free Traders,
especially on a Class D ship such as the *Lydis*, are not given
to many second thoughts. We are of an exploring fraternity,
willing to run risks in order to work among our own kind.
Did Foss suspect something which was not clear to the rest
of us? The fact that he even suggested that the ship not
resume her voyage to Ptah after the necessary repairs was
suspicious. Yet after we were alone, making a recorder copy
of all matters pertaining to the contract, Lidj did not com-
ment. And since he did not, I was silent also.

By early morning we had our tape ready as the Patrol
flitter came gliding over the barrier of the valley wall and
stirred up ashy sand in landing beside the *Lydis*. The two
men who climbed out of the small flyer appeared to be in
no great hurry to join Foss, who stood at the foot of our
downed ramp. Instead one knelt in the sand, setting up an
instrument. And the other watched him closely. They could
have been conducting an exploring survey.

Chapter 6

KRIP VORLUND

There is something about the cloak of authority which tends to put even the citizen with a clear conscience on the defensive. So it was when we fronted the representatives of the Patrol. As law-abiding and inoffensive space traders, making regular contributions to planetary landing taxes, all papers in order, we had every right to call upon their help. It was just that they eyed us with an impassivity which suggested that to them, everything had to be proved twice over.

However, we had the box taken from the Throne of Qur carefully disinterred after they admitted that their own instruments registered emanations of a heretofore unknown radiation. It was surrendered gladly to their custody, along with the body of the priest, which had been in freeze. And we each entered testimony on the truth tape, which could not be tampered with.

With relief we knew they had not asked all the questions they might have. Our find at the cat cliff was still our secret

—though we did tell of the cargo cache. Lidj, armed with all the precedents of space law, explained that once repairs were made, we intended to continue our voyage and deliver the treasure to the temple on Ptah—providing we were sure that the priests to whom it was officially consigned were still in power.

"We have no news from Ptah." The pilot of the Scout displayed so little interest in Foss's inquiries it was plain our present dilemma was of no concern to him. "Your repairs, yes. Our engineer has checked with your man. We want visa-tapes of the damage for our report. We can lift you and your engineer off to our space base, where you can indite under League contract for what you need."

Indite under League contract was a suggestion to worry one, though here we had no alternative. Once we had so indited we would be answerable not to the Patrol, but to our own people. Not to pay up within the stated time meant having the *Lydis* put under bond. There was so great a demand for ships (men waited for frustrating years for some stroke of luck which would give them even the first step on the ladder of spacing) that bonds weighed heavily on those who had to accept them. They could mean the loss of a ship. So we had no way of recouping, save that of delivering our cargo to Ptah, hoping to collect. That—or the wild chance that the cat cliff hid something worth the labor of breaking in. We had no time now to build a probe, nor could we do that without giving away the reason.

In the end it was decided that Foss and Shallard would lift with the Scout. But an armed party of Patrol, plus their flitter, would remain on Sekhmet, their first order being to search for our missing men.

Since the Patrol flitter was a heavy-duty craft, armed and
protected by every device known, it might have a better
chance in a search. It carried a pilot, two gunners to man
its shockers, and room for two more passengers. There was
no drawing of lots this time. Before he took off for the
Scout Foss spoke directly to me.

"You and Maelen will go. With her powers to search and
yours to interpret—"

Of course he was right, though the Patrolman regarded
his choice of what appeared to be an animal with open
disbelief. However, though I gave no history of Maelen's
past, I laid it out clearly that she was telepathic and would
be our guide. Since no man may know all there is to be
learned about alien creatures, they accepted my assurance
of her worth.

For a full day after the Scout lifted with Captain Foss
and Shallard, there was a storm lapping at the *Lydis*, raising
the fine dust of the valley into an impenetrable fog, keeping
us pent within the ship, the Patrolmen with us. There was
no setting out in this murk, since we could not fly on any
set beam but would be questing freely over an unknown
area.

But on the second morning the wind failed. And though
the ash-sand had drifted high about the fins of the ship and
half buried the flitter, which was well anchored in what
little protection the *Lydis* herself offered, we could take off.
As we swung out over the knife-ridged country, the massed
clouds overhead broke a little now and then, though the
sunlight which came through was pale and seemed devoid
of heat. Its radiance accentuated the general gloom of the
landscape beneath us rather than dispersing it.

The pilot kept to the lowest speed, watching his instruments for any sign of radiation which might be promising. Maelen crouched beside me in the cramped cabin of the craft. It was seldom I was truly aware of her present form, but with the Patrolmen glancing at her as if she were a very outré piece of equipment, I was more conscious of her fur, her four feet, the glassia guise. And because I had heard her plaint of fear, that she might in time slide back too far into the animal to be sure of her identity as a Thassa, her unease was plainer to me. I myself had known moments when beast eclipsed man. What if my identity had been so lost?

Maelen was stronger, more prepared than I had been to overpower the flesh envelope she wore, since she knew well all its dangers. But if *her* steady confidence was beginning to fade—

She stirred, muscles moving with liquid grace under her soft fur. Her head pointed away in a quick turn.

"Something?" I asked.

"Not what I seek now. But—but there is that down there which is not of rock and sand."

I craned to look through the vision port. Nothing showed to my sight, but rocks twisted and eroded into such wild shapes could hide anything.

"Within—" she informed me. "But we are already past. I think perhaps another cache—"

I tried to memorize landmarks, though such seen from the air and from the ground were two different matters. But if Maelen was right, and her certainty of report suggested that she could be depended upon to be that, perhaps we had indeed come upon that which would redeem all debts we might incur through this trouble. A second cache! Was Sekhmet to prove as rich a treasure field as Thoth—perhaps more so?

However, Maelen reported nothing else as we flew in a zigzag pattern, cruising back and forth over the broken land. The country was bad for visual sighting. There were too many of those deep, narrow valleys which might have swallowed up a grounded or crashed flitter, hiding it even from air survey. And we knew only the general direction.

Back and forth, as all the rocks took on the same look—though we did pass over several wider valleys where there were stands of withered vegetation. One held a cup of water in the form of a small, dark lake rimmed with a wide border of yellow-white which may have been a noxious chemical deposit.

Maelen stirred again, pressing more tightly against me, as she stretched her head toward the vision port.

"What now?"

"Life—" she signaled.

At the same time our pilot leaned forward to regard more closely one of the many dials before him.

"Reading—faint radiation," he reported.

Though we were already at a low altitude, he dropped us more, at the same time cutting speed nearly to hover so we could search with care through the vision port. We were heading over one of the valleys, which was roughly half-moon-shaped. At the upper point of that were the first trees (if trees one might term them) I had yet seen on Sekhmet. At least they were growths of very dark foliage which stood well above bush level. But the rest of the ground was covered only with the gray tough grass.

"There!"

There was no need for anyone to point it out—for it
was as visible as if painted scarlet. A flitter stood in grass
as high as its hatch. But there were no signs of life about it.

The pilot had been calling on his com, trying to raise an
answer. As yet he made no move to set down. I did not
wonder at his caution. There was something about the stark
loneliness of that valley, about the seemingly deserted
machine so plainly in sight, which chilled me.

"Do you pick them up?" I asked Maelen.

"There is no one right here." By that she seemed to
contradict her earlier report.

"But you said—"

"It is not them. Something else—" Her thought-send
faltered, almost as if she were now confused, unable to
sense clearly.

And my uneasiness, which had been triggered by the
sight of the parked flitter, was fed by a suspicion that perhaps this was what Maelen had obliquely warned me of
earlier, that she could no longer be sure of her powers.

"Snooper picks up nothing," the pilot reported. "I don't
get any ident reading. By all tests there's no one aboard."

"Only one way to make sure," commented the Patrolman
at the port-side defense. "Set down and look."

"I don't like it. Looks almost as if it were put out for
someone to come and see it." The pilot's hand had not
yet gone to the controls. "Bait—"

That was a possibility one could readily accept. Though
who would be using such bait? With the Patrol insignia
plain on our own craft, it would be top risk for anyone to
spring a trap. Perhaps my faith in the force of the Patrol

was right, for we did come down. Though both gunners stayed at their posts as we flattened the high grass not too far from the parked flitter.

The grass was not only close to chest-high, but tough and sharp-edged, cutting any hand put out to beat it down. Yet it also gave us a clue as to what might have happened to the two we sought. For the flitter was empty of any passengers. Not only that, but their supply packs were still stowed within, as if Sharvan and Hunold had never expected to leave the flyer for long.

Out from the trampled and crushed section of grass immediately around the hatch a trail led straight for the stand of trees. The path was deeply indented, as though it might have been made by the transportation of heavy cargo. Yet here and there along it tougher patches of stem and leaf were lifting again.

I searched the flitter carefully, triggering its report tape. But that repeated nothing more in its last recording than a description of what we ourselves had seen during our morning's passage over the broken lands. Then it stopped in mid-word, the rest of the tape as bare as if it had been erased. For this I had no explanation at all. Whatever had brought them to land here remained a mystery. Still, all the instruments were in working order. I was able to apply full power and raise to a good height in testing before I set down again. There had been no failure of the craft to force a landing.

As I made my examination one of the Patrol gunners and the pilot, Harkon, went for some distance down the trail leading to the trees. Maelen remained behind, hunkered

down at the edge of the slowly rising grass. And as I
emerged from the hatch I had one question for her.

"How long?"

She sniffed the ground in the trampled space, using
glassia gifts now.

"More than a day. Perhaps as long as they have been
missing. I cannot be too sure. Krip—there is a strange
scent here—human. Come—"

A swing of her head beckoned me to one side and there
she used the unsheathed claws of one forepaw to pull aside
the tall grass. The tuft did not come easily and I put out
my mittened hands to help. Then I found the vegetation
had been woven into a blind, forming a screen about a
space where the ground had been grubbed clear. Upon the
patch of soil was the impression of a square which might
have been left by a heavy box.

I had knelt to examine this depression as the Patrolmen
returned. Harkon joined me. He held a small detect and I
heard a revealing chatter from that.

"Small residue of radiation. Could be left from something like a call beam," he commented. Then he studied
the woven grass curtain. "Well hidden—this could not have
been spotted from above at all. They could even have produced engine failure and at the same time blotted out a
distress signal—"

"But why?"

"You people have already claimed sabotage. Well, if
your men had reached the beacon they could have spoiled
any game to be played here. It was only by chance we
picked up your space call, one chance in five hundred,

really. Whoever is in hiding here could not have foreseen that. Or even that your com-tech had the knowledge and equipment to try it. If they have a reason to keep you pinned here, the first step would be to cut you off from the beacon. And they must believe that by taking your flitter, they have done that effectively. And as to who 'they' are—" He shrugged. "You ought to have some guess."

"Outside of jacks with inside knowledge about our cargo —no. But what about Sharvan and Hunold?"

I meant that question as much for Maelen as Harkon, and I thought she might have the more reliable answer.

"They were alive when they left here," she replied.

"No attempt made to conceal the trail. I don't think they believed anyone would be after them in a hurry," Harkon replied when I passed along Maelen's report.

"You have this much reassurance," he added. "The Free Traders' loyalty to their own is a known fact. They might keep your men alive to bargain with."

"Exchange." I nodded. "But we have had no offers— nothing. No one we could detect has been near the *Lydis*."

"Which is not to say that they won't show up with a ransom deal sooner or later."

I arose, brushing the dead grass wisps from my thermo suit. "Maybe not now. Not if they saw your ship land."

Yet jacks are not timid, not when they have such a rich take as the *Lydis*'s cargo to consider. The Patrol ship was a Scout, and it had gone off-world again. Three Patrolmen in an armed flitter, and the reduced crew of the *Lydis*— This might be the very time the enemy would select to make such a move, if they did have us under observation. I said as much.

"We'll follow the trail to the woods anyway," Harkon answered. "If there's nothing beyond"— he shrugged again —"nothing to do then but wait for reinforcements. We can't stand up to a jack gang with only three men."

I noted that he apparently did not class the Free Traders as part of his fighting force. But perhaps to the Patrol any outside their own close company was not to be so considered. Just another of the things which made them less than popular.

We left one gunner on guard and tramped along the grass track once more, Maelen with me now, Harkon ahead, his fellow bringing up the rear. As we drew near that wood I saw that the growths could indeed be termed trees, but they lacked any attraction, their limbs being twisted and coiled as if they had once been supple tentacles flung out in a wild attempt to embrace something and had solidified in such ungainly positions. The leaves were very dark and thick-fleshed, and there were not many to a limb. But they were still able to form a heavy canopy which shut out that pallid sunlight and made the way ahead a tunnel of deep dusk.

But the path we followed did not enter there. Instead it turned left to run along the edge of the stand. Here there was little grass, but the gray soil showed scrapes and scuffs, being too soft to retain sharp prints. Having skirted the woods, the way came to the very point of the valley. Maelen, who had paced by my side, drew away to the sharp rise of the cliff.

She sat up on her haunches, her head swaying a little; she might almost have been reading some inscription carved on that rugged wall, so intently did she regard it. I took a couple of strides to join her, but I could see nothing, though I searched, believing that she must have come upon something such as the cat mask.

"What is it now?" I ventured to break her concentration.

For the first time she made no answer. Her mind was closed as tight as any defense gate barred to the enemy. Still she stared, her head turning a fraction right, left, right again. But I could detect nothing to keep her so scanning stone.

"What is it?" Harkon echoed my question.

"I don't know. Maelen does not answer." I touched the raised crest on her head.

She drew back from even that small physical contact. Nor did she open her mind or show that she was aware of me. Never before had this happened.

"Maelen!" I made of her name a challenge, a demand for attention. And I thought that even so I had not reached her. That fear she had implanted in me, the suggestion that she might surrender to her beast body, was sharp.

Then that swinging of the head, the unblinking stare, broke. I saw her red tongue flick out, lick her muzzle. Both her forepaws scraped upward along the sides of her head in a gesture which aped the human. She might have been trying to close her ears to some sound she could no longer stand, which was racking her with pain.

"Maelen!" I went to my knees. Our eyes were now nearly level. Putting out my hand, I caught those paws holding her head, urged her face a little around to meet my gaze. She blinked and blinked again—almost as one rousing from sleep.

"Maelen, what is the matter?"

There was no longer that solid barrier. Rather I was answered by a flood of confused impressions which I could not easily sort out. Then she steadied her chain of thought.

"Krip—I must get away—away from here!"

"Danger?"

"Yes—at least to me. But not from those we seek. There is something else. It has prowled at the edge of my thoughts since first we set foot on this dark world. Krip, if I do not take care there is that here which can claim me! I am Thassa—I am mistress—" I felt she did not say that to me, but repeated the words to herself to steady her control. "I am Thassa!"

"You are Thassa!" Straightway I hastened to say that, as if merely repeating my conviction would be a life line thrown to one struggling against dire danger.

She dropped her forepaws to earth. Now her whole body was shaken by great shudders, such as might result from violent weeping. I dared to touch her again, and when, this time, she did not repulse me, I drew her close for such companionship as that hold might give her.

"You are Maelen of the Thassa." I held my thought firm. "As you will ever be! Nothing else can claim you here. It cannot!"

"What is the matter?" Harkon's hand was on my shoulder, giving me a small shake as if to summon my attention.

"I do not know." I told him the truth. "There is something here that threatens esper powers."

"Harkon!" The other Patrolman, who had gone along the cliff, now stepped away from it. "Set-down marks here. A flitter—big one by the looks of them."

Harkon went to see; I remained with Maelen. She had turned her head, was nuzzling against my jacket in an intimacy she had never before displayed.

"Good—good to have you here," her thought came. "Keep so, Krip, keep so with me. I must not be less nor other than I am—I must not! But it is calling—it is calling me—"

"What is?"

"I do not know. It is like something which wishes help that only I can offer. Yet I also know that if I do go to it— then I am no longer me. And I will not be not-Maelen! Never while I live will I be not-Maelen!" The force of that was like a shout of defiance.

"No one but Maelen. Tell me how I can aid. I am here—" I gave her quickly what I had to offer.

"Remember Maelen, Krip, remember Maelen!"

I guessed what she wanted and built in my mind the picture I liked to remember best of all—of Maelen as I had first seen her at the Great Fair in Yrjar, serene, sure, mistress of herself, untroubled, proud of her little furred people as they performed before the awed townsfolk. That was Maelen as she would always be for me.

"Did you indeed see me so, Krip? I think you draw a picture larger and more comely, more assured, than I was in truth. But you have given me that to hold to. Keep it ever for me, Krip. When I need it—have it safe!"

Harkon was back. "Nothing more to do here." His tone was impatient. "We had better head back. They lifted in a flitter, all right, which means they can be anywhere on this continent. Can you pilot your own flyer?"

I nodded, but looked to Maelen. Was she ready, able, to return? She wriggled in my hold and I loosed her. Perhaps she was well pleased to be on the move again. She scrambled into the flitter, curled up in the second seat as I settled in front of the controls.

The Patrol flitter headed straight back toward the *Lydis* and I matched its speed. Maelen, curled still, seemed to sleep. At least she made no attempt at mind-touch. However, we were not to be long without a new problem. My com clicked and I snapped it on.

"Can you raise your ship?" was Harkon's terse demand.

I had been so absorbed with Maelen I had not thought of sending any report to the *Lydis*. Now I pressed the broadcast button. There was a hum—the beam was open. But when I punched out our code call I got no answer. Surprised, I tried again. The beam *was* open; reception should have been easy. Surely with us out on search the ship's receiver would have been constantly manned. Still no reply.

I reported my failure to Harkon, to be answered with a stark "Same here."

We had set out in early morning, eating our midday meal of concentrates as we flew. Now began a fading of the pallid sunlight, a thickening and indrawing of the clouds. Also the winds were rising. For safety's sake we both rose well above the rocky hills. There was no way we could be lost—the guide beam would pull us to the *Lydis*—but strong winds might make a blind landing there tricky. A blind landing? It should not have to be blind. They would be expecting us, have floodlights out to guide us down. Or

would they? They did not answer—would they even know
we were coming? *Why* did I get no answer? I continued to
click out the code call, pausing now and then to count to
ten or twenty, praying for an answer which would end my
rising suspicion that something was very wrong.

Chapter 7

MAELEN

It was hard to fight this thing which had come upon me in the valley where we found the flitter. Never had I been so shaken, so unsure of myself, of what I was—of *who* I was. Yet I could not even remember clearly now that which had flowed in upon my mind, possessing my thoughts, struggling to eject my identity. I know shape-changing, who better? But this was no ordered way of Thassa doing. This had been a concentrated attempt to force me to action which was not of my own planning.

As I crouched low now in the second seat of the flitter, I was still trying to draw about me, as one might draw a ragged cloak against the stabbing air of winter, my confidence and belief in my own powers. What I had met there I could not trace to its source and did not know—save that I wanted no more of it!

I was thus so intent upon my own misery and fear that I was not wholly aware of Krip's actions. Until his thought came piercing my self-absorption in a quick, clean thrust.

"Maelen! They do not reply from the *Lydis*. What can you read?"

Read? For a moment even his mind-send seemed to be in a different language, one beyond my comprehension. Then I drew heavily on my control, forced my thought away from that dire contact in the valley. *Lydis*—the *Lydis* did not answer!

But at least now I had a concrete focus for my search. I was not battling the unknown. Though the ship itself, being inanimate, would not act as a guide to draw my search; Lidj would be best for that. I pictured in my mind the cargomaster, loosed my tendril of seek—

What I encountered was a blank. No—below the surface of nothingness there pulsed something, a very muted sense of identity. I have mind-sought when those I so wished to touch were asleep, even in deep unconsciousness produced by illness. This present state was like unto the last, save that it was even deeper, farther below the conscious level. Lidj was not to be reached by any seek of mine. I transferred then to Korde—with the same result.

"They are unconscious—Lidj and Korde—deeply so," I reported.

"Asleep!"

"Not true sleep. I have reported it as it is. They are not conscious, nor do they dream, nor are their minds open to under-thought as they are in true sleep. This is something else."

I tried to probe deeper, to awaken some response, enough to win information. But even as I concentrated I was— seized! It was as if I had been pushing toward a goal when about me rose a trapping net. This net had the same feel as that which had entranced me for a space in the valley. Save that this time it was stronger, held me more rigidly in its bonds, as if another personality, stronger, more compelling, had joined with the first to bind and draw me. I could see Krip and the flitter. I could look down at my own furred body, at my forepaws, from which the striking claws were now protruding as if I were preparing to do battle. But between me and that sane outer world there was building a wall of haze.

Maelen—I was Maelen! "Krip, think me Maelen as you did in the valley! Make me see myself as I truly am, have been all my life, no matter what body I now wear. I am Maelen!"

However, my plea must not have reached him. I was dimly aware of a crackle of words from the com, words which had noise but no meaning.

Maelen—with all my strength of mind and will I held to my need of identity, besieged by rising waves of force, each beating upon me stronger than the last. Dimly I thought this a worse peril because I *was* one who had been able to change the outward coverings of my spirit—something which made me the more susceptible to whatever abode here.

But—I was Maelen—not Vors, no one else—only Maelen of the Thassa. Now my world had narrowed to that single piece of knowledge, which was my shield, or my weapon. Maelen as Krip had seen me in his memory. Though, as I had told him, I had never been so fair, so strong as that. Maelen—

All beyond me was gone now. I closed my outer eyes lest I be disturbed from my defense. For how long I continued then to hold Maelen intact I do not know, as time was no longer broken down into any unit of measure. It was only endurance in which I feared weakening more than any bodily death.

That assault grew in strength, reached such a height that I knew if it advanced I could not hold. Then—it began to fail. With failure there came a secondary current, first of raging impatience, then of fear and despair. This time also I had held fast. That I could do so a third time with this strange power fighting against me, I doubted. And Krip— where had Krip been? What of his promise that he would stand with me?

Anger born of my great fear flared hot in me. Was this the true worth of what I might expect from him, that in my hour of greatest need he would leave me to fight a lone battle?

The influence which had tested me this second time was now gone, the remnants winking out as a lamp might give way to the dark. I was left so drained that I could not move, even once I had returned to an awareness of what lay about me.

Krip—he still sat at the controls of the flitter. But the flyer was on the ground. I could see from the vision port the fins of the *Lydis,* though the bulk of the ship towered far above us.

"Krip—" Weakly I tried to reach him.

Tried—but what I met was that same nothingness which I had encountered when I had sought Lidj and Korde! I pulled up on the seat, edged around to look directly into his face.

His eyes were open; he stared straight ahead. I reached

out a forepaw, caught at his shoulder. His body was rigid, as if frozen, a piece of carving rather than blood, flesh, and bone! Had he been caught in that same net which had tried to encompass me, but more securely?

I began to fight again, this time to reach that which lay beneath the weight of nothingness. But I was too weakened by my own ordeal—I could not win to that secret place where Krip Vorlund had been imprisoned, or to which he had retreated. He sat rigid, frozen, staring with eyes I did not believe saw anything of the outer world. I scrambled off the seat, clumsily freed the catch of the door hatch with my paws.

Though the fins of the *Lydis* were bulky enough to show through the dark, the rest of the valley was well hidden in night shadows. I dropped over the edge of the hatch into the soft sand, which puffed up around my haunches, cushioning me by the edge of a dune. The hatch closed automatically behind me. Krip had not noticed my going, made no effort to join me.

Standing in the shadow cast by the flitter, I surveyed the valley. There was no boarding ramp out from the *Lydis*. She was locked tight, as we had kept her during each night on Sekhmet. Beyond the fins was the Patrol flitter. Around that was no stir. I padded through the sand to reach its side. There was a faint glow within, the radiance of the instrument panel, I thought.

Glassia can climb, but they are no leapers. Now I made a great effort, putting all I could into a jump which allowed me to hook my claws over the edge of the port, hang there long enough with a straining of my shoulder muscles for a look within.

The pilot occupied his seat with the same rigidity Krip displayed. His nearest companion was in position by the weapon, also frozen at his post. I could only see the back of the head of the second gunner, but since he did not move, I believed I could assume he was in a like state. Both the pilot and Krip had made good landings here, but now they seemed as truly prisoners as if they were chained in some dungeon in Yrjar. Prisoners of whom—and why? Still, since they had landed their flitters in safety, it was plain that the enemy did not yet want them dead, only under control.

That they would be left so for long, I doubted. And prudence suggested that I get into hiding while I could and stay so until I learned more of the situation. I might already be under surveillance from some point in the valley.

I began to test mind-seek—only to find it limited, so drawn upon by the ordeal I had been through that I dared not try it far. For the time being I was reduced to depending upon the five senses inherent in my present body.

Though it disturbed me to rely on the glassia abilities, I relaxed my vigilance and my control of my body, raised my head so that my nose could test the scents in the air, listened as intently as I could, tried to see as much among the shadows as my eyes would allow. The glassia are not nocturnal. Their night vision is probably but little better than a man's. But the contrast of the light-gray sand with the flitters and the tall bulk of the *Lydis* was enough to give me my bearings. And if I could reach the cliff wall, its rugged formation would offer me hiding in plenty. I squatted in the shadow of the Patrol flitter and mapped out a route which would give me maximum cover.

Perhaps I was wasting time; perhaps the valley was not under observation and I could have walked boldly enough. But that was too chancy. So I covered the ground with all the craft I could summon, alert to any sight or noise which could mean I was betrayed.

Then I found a crevice I thought was promising. It was so narrow that I must back into it. Within that I crouched, lying low, my head resting on my paws, taking up vigil to watch the ship and the two flitters.

As during that pallid day before, the clouds parted a little. There were stars to be seen, but no moon. I thought with longing of the bright glow of Sotrath, which gave such light to Yiktor, filling the night with blazing splendor.

Stars above me—or were they? For a beast, distances are altered, angles of vision changed. Not stars—lights! Those lower ones at least were lights, at one end of the valley. Three I counted. And in that direction was the spot where we had cached the cargo. With the crew and the Patrolmen caught now, were those mysterious others we suspected to be at the root of our troubles working to loot the treasure?

Having established the presence of the lights, I caught something else which came through the rocks about me—a vibration. Nothing stirred in the valley, there was no sign of any watcher. Perhaps whoever had set this trap had been so confident of its holding for as long as necessary that no sentry had been posted. I squirmed uneasily. I did not in the least want to do what I thought must be done—go to see if my suspicions were correct, that the cache was being looted—to see who was responsible. Stubbornly I hunkered in what seemed to me now to be a shell of safety, one I would be worse than foolish to leave.

I owed no allegiance to the *Lydis*. I was no Free Trader. Krip—Krip Vorlund. Yes, there was a tie between us I had no thought or wish to break. But for the rest— Yet Krip had as strong ties to them, so I was bound to their fate whether I would or no. Could a glassia have sighed, I would have done so then as I most reluctantly crawled out of my safe little pocket and began to pad along at the foot of the cliff, making use once more of every bit of cover.

When I had gone exploring with Krip we had suited our path to the demands of his human body. But I knew I could take a much faster way up and over the heights, since my powerful claws were well fitted to climbing this rock riddled with cracks and crevices. I worked my way around until I reached a spot which I thought directly in line with those lights. There I began to climb. The rock face was dark enough so that my black fur would not show against its surface as it would have on the light dunes. As I had hoped, my claws readily found and clung to irregularities which served me well.

I made better speed at this than I had skulking about on the ground, and so managed to pull out on top of the ridge hardly winded by my efforts. From this vantage point I could see my suspicions were in part true. Three lights, giving from here a greater glow of illumination, were at the point where Foss and the others had thought they had so well hidden the cargo. Yet the effort of breaking through the plug they had left there could not be an easy one. I guessed from the vibration in the rocks, and a faint purr of sound now to be heard, that some machine had been brought in to handle that task.

So intent had I been on that distant work I was not at first aware of what lay closer. Not until I moved a little aside and edged against that beam— Shock struck me with the power of a blow. Had I met it at a point of greater intensity I might actually have been borne back to crash into the valley.

It was pure force, delivered with such strength that one could believe such a beam should be visible. And it was mind force. Yet this was a concentration I had never experienced, even when our Old Ones merged their power for some needful action. That it had to do with the blanked minds of the humans below, I had no doubt at all. I was prepared now, wary, my defenses up, so that I could skirt the danger and not be once more entrapped. And that I must find the source, I also knew.

I did not want a second meeting with that deadly beam, yet I must somehow keep in contact in order to trace it. So I was reduced to flinching in and out on the edge, reeling away, shuffling on to touch again. Thus I came to a niche in the rocks. There was no light there, no one around; I summoned up enough mind-seek to make sure before I approached that pocket from the rear. It was very dark and whatever was in there was deeply set back in the niche.

Finally I had to pull my way to the top of the rock pile, since I had made sure that the only opening lay at the front. Crouched with my belly flat on the arch, I clawed myself forward. Then I bent my head down, hoping that the beam did not fill the whole of the opening, that I could see what lay inside.

It had seemed dark when viewed from a distance. But

within the very narrow space was a faint glimmer, enough
to reveal the occupant. I was looking, from a cramped,
upside-down position, into a face!

The shock of that nearly loosed me from my precarious
hold. I regained control, was able to concentrate on those
set, grim features. The eyes of the stranger were shut, his
face utterly expressionless, as if he slept. And his body was
enclosed in a box which had been wedged upright so that
he faced out over the valley. The main part of the box was
frosted, so that only the section of cover directly over his
face was clear. The face was humanoid enough, though
completely hairless, without even brows or lashes. And the
skin was a pale gray.

The box which enclosed him (I believed the sleeper to
be male) was equipped with a front panel which might
have been transparent had not the frosted condition pre-
vailed, for it looked like crystal. This was banded by a
wide frame of metal flecked here and there with small
specks of color I could not see clearly.

At the foot of the box was another piece of equipment.
And while the sleeper (if sleeper he was) resembled nothing
I had seen before, what sat at his feet was familiar. I had
seen its like employed only a few days ago in the *Lydis*. It
was an amplifier for communication, such as Korde had
rigged when he made the off-world distress call.

Seeing it where it now was left only one inference to be
drawn. The mind-blast was coming from the boxed body,
to be amplified by the com device. Also, its being here could
have only one purpose—that of holding Krip, the Patrolmen, and presumably the crew of the *Lydis* in thrall. Could

I in some manner disconnect it, or abate the flow of current, they might be released.

About the boxed sleeper I could do nothing. I was not strong enough to handle the case—it had been too tightly wedged into that niche. My eyes, adjusting to the very faint light emitted from the frame, showed that rocks had been pounded in about the large box to pin it in place.

So—I might not get at the source of the mind-thrall, but the amplifier was another matter. I remembered well how cautiously Korde had adjusted the one on the *Lydis*, his constant warning that the slightest jar could deflect the line of force beam. But this was a task I had to push myself to. For, just as I had tired under my battle in the flitter with that which had tried to take over my mind, so now did my body send messages of distress through aching muscles, fatigue-heavy limbs.

I withdrew to the ground below and moved in cautiously from the side, creeping low and so hoping to elude the full force of the beam. Luckily it did not appear to sweep the ground.

Having made this discovery, I found it easy to wriggle closer. I could see only one possible way, and success would depend upon just how clumsy this animal body was. Backing off, I went to look for a weapon. But here the scouring winds had done their work far too well. There were no loose stones small enough to serve me. I padded along, nosing into every hole I saw, becoming more and more desperate. If I had to return to the floor of the valley to search, I would. But I still hoped.

Stubbornness rewarded me in the end, for in one of the

hollows I found a rock which I worried at with my claws
until it loosened, so that I could scrape it out into the open.
When one has always been served by hands, it is difficult
to use one's mouth. But I got the rock between my teeth
and returned.

Once more I edged in as flat as I could, and with the
stone between my teeth I hammered away at the top of the
amplifier, until that was so battered I did not believe those
who had left it could ever use it again.

I did not approach the box of the sleeper. But from that
seeped a dank chill, like the worst blast of highland winter
I had ever met on Yiktor. I believed that had I set paw to
that frosted front, I might well have frozen a limb by that
unwary touch. There was no change in the face, which
could have been that of a carven statue. Yet the sleeper
lived, or had once lived. Looking up at the entombed
stirred a confused feeling in me.

Quickly I not only glanced away from those set features,
but also backed out of the line of sight of the closed eyes.
The other, added presence I had sensed in the flitter—I felt
a stirring of that. And the sensation caused such alarm in
me that I loped away without heeding the direction of my
going.

When I had my emotions once more under control, and
that hint of troubling influence was gone, I discovered I had
headed not back to the ship valley but toward the lights and
the purr of sound. It might be well for me to scout that
scene of activity. I hoped that now that the broadcast had
been stopped, those in the *Lydis* and flitters would be free.
And it could be to their advantage if I were able to supply
information upon my return.

The strangers had no guards or sentries about. Perhaps they were so certain of that which they had put to work in the heights that they felt safe. And it was easy enough to slip up to a good vantage point.

Busy at the cache they were, with flares lighting the scene, brighter even than Sekhmet's daylight. Robos, two of them, were at work on the plug we had set to seal the crevice. But the Traders had done so good a job there that the machines were not breaking it down in any hurry. They had various tools, flamers, and the like fitted into their work sockets and were attacking the fused stone with vigor.

The robos of the *Lydis* were mainly for loading, although in extreme need they could be equipped with a few simple working tool modifications. These looked larger and different. They were being directed to their labor by a man holding a control board. And, though I knew little of such machines, I thought they seemed chiefly intended for excavation work.

As far as we of the *Lydis* knew, there were no mines on Sekhmet. And casual prospectors did not own such elaborate and costly machines. We had found traces of what might be treasure deposits here. Could these robos have been imported to open such deposits?

The men below—there were three of them—looked like any spacers, wearing the common coveralls of ship crewmen. They appeared completely humanoid, of the same stock as the Free Traders. The two who were not controlling the robos carried weapons, blasters to be exact, an indication that they could well be outside the law. The sight of those was warning enough for me to keep my distance.

I stiffened against the ground, my breath hissing between those fangs which were a glassia's natural weapons. A fourth man had come into sight. And his face was very clear in the flare lamps. It was Griss Sharvan!

There were no signs of his being a prisoner. He stopped beside one of the guards, watching the robos with as much interest as if he had set them to work. Had he? Was it Sharvan who had led this crew to the cache? But why? It was very hard for anyone who knew the Traders to believe that one of them could turn traitor to his kind. Their loyalty was inbred. I would have sworn by all I knew that such a betrayal was totally impossible. Yet there he stood, seemingly on excellent terms with the looters.

From time to time the robo master made adjustments on the controls. I caught a feeling of impatience from him. And when that reached my conscious attention, I thought that the weakening of my power had passed. Which meant I might just dare to discover, via mind-probe, what Sharvan did here. Settling myself to the easiest position I could find, I began probe.

Chapter 8

KRIP VORLUND

It was very quiet; there was no *thrum* in the walls, no feeling of the usual safe containment which a ship gave. I opened my eyes—but not upon the walls of my cabin in the *Lydis*; instead I was facing the control board of a flitter. And as I blinked, more than a little bemused, recollection flowed in. The last thing I could remember clearly was flying over the broken ranges on my way back to the ship.

But I was not flying now. Then how had I landed, and—

I turned to look at the second seat. There was no furred body there. And a quick survey told me that I was alone in the flitter. Yet surely Maelen could not have landed us. And the dark outside was now that of night.

It took only an instant or two to open the hatch and stumble out of the flyer. Beside me rose the *Lydis*. Beyond her I could make out a second flitter. But why could I not remember? What had happened just before we landed?

"Vorlund!" My name out of the night.

"Who's there?"

"Harkon." A dark shadow came from the other flitter, plowed through the sand toward me.

"How did we get here?" he demanded. But I could not give him any answer to that.

There was a grating sound from the ship. I raised my head to see the ramp issue from her upper hatch like a tongue thrust out to explore. Moments later its end thudded to earth only a short distance away. But I was more intent on finding Maelen.

The sand around held no prints; I could not pick up a trail. But if the ship's ramp had been up, she could not have gone aboard. I could not imagine what would have taken her away from the flitter. Except her strange actions back in that other valley made me wonder if some influence had drawn her beyond her powers of resistance. If so, what influence, and why would it affect her more here? Also, I could not remember landing the flitter—

I flashed out a mind-seek. And an instant later I reeled back, striking against the body of the flitter I had just quitted, going to my knees, my hands against my head, unable to think clearly, gasping for breath—for—

By the time Harkon reached me I must have been very close to complete blackout. I recall only dimly being led on board the *Lydis*, people moving about me. Then I choked, gasped, shook my head as strong fumes cut through the frightening mist which was between me and the world. I looked up, able to see and recognize what I saw—the sick bay of the ship. Medic Lukas was by me, backed by Lidj and Harkon.

"What—what happened?"

"You tell us," Lukas said.

My head—I turned it a little on the pillow. That sicken-
ing wave of assaulting blackness mixed with pain ebbed.

"Maelen—she was gone. I tried to find her by mind-seek.
Then—something hit—inside my head." It was as hard
now to describe the nature of that attack as it was to
remember how I had come earlier to land the flitter.

"It agrees." Lukas nodded. But what agreed with what,
no one explained to me. Until he continued, "Esper force
stepped up to that degree can register as energy." He
shook his head. "I would have said it was impossible, except
on one world or another the impossible is often proved
true."

"Esper," I repeated. My head ached now, with a degree
of pain which made me rather sick. Maelen, what about
her? But perhaps to try mind-seek again would bring
another such attack, and that dread was realized as Lukas
continued:

"Keep away from the use of that, Krip. At least until we
know more of what is happening. You had such a dose of
energy that you were nearly knocked out."

"Maelen—she's gone!"

He did not quite meet my eyes then. I thought I could
guess what he was thinking.

"She wasn't responsible! I know her sending—"

"Then who did?" Harkon demanded. "You stated from
the start that she is highly telepathic. Well, this is being
done by a telepath of unusual talent and perhaps training.
And I would like to know who landed us here—since we
cannot remember! Were we taken over by your animal?"

"No!" I struggled to sit up, and then doubled over,
fighting the nausea and feeling of disorientation that move-

ment caused. Lukas put something quickly to my mouth
and I sucked at a tube, swallowing cool liquid which allayed
the sickness.

"It was *not* Maelen!" I got out when I finished that
potion. "You cannot mistake a mind sending—it is as
individual as a voice, a face. This—this was alien." Now
that I had had a few moments in which to think about it,
I knew that was true.

"Also"—Lukas turned to Lidj— "tell them what registered on our receivers here."

"We have a recording," the cargomaster began. "This
esper attack began some time ago—and you were not here
then. It broke in intensity about a half hour since—dropped
far down the scale, though it still registers. Just as if some
transmission of energy had been brought to a peak and then
partly shut off. While it was on at the top range none of
us can remember anything. We must have awakened, if
you can term it that, at the moment it dropped. But the
residue remaining is apparently enough to knock out anyone trying esper communication, as Krip proved. So if it
was not Maelen—"

"But where is she now?" I swallowed experimentally as I
raised my head, and discovered I felt better. "I was alone
in the flitter when I awoke—and no one can find a trail
through that sand out there."

"It may be that she has gone to hunt the source of what
hit us. She is a far greater esper than any of our breed,"
Lidj suggested.

I pulled myself up, pushing away Lukas's hand when he
put it out to deter me. "Or else she was drawn unwillingly.
She felt something back there in that valley where we found

the flitter, she begged me to get her away. She—she may have been caught by whatever is there!"

"It is not going to help her to go charging out without any idea of what you may be up against." Lidj's good sense might not appeal to me then, but since he, Lukas, and Harkon made a barrier at the door of the sick bay I was sure I was not going to get past them at present.

"If you think I am going to stay safe in here while—" I began. Lidj shook his head.

"I am only saying that we have to know more about the enemy before we go into battle. We have had enough warning to be sure that this is something we have never faced before. And what good will it do Maelen, Sharvan, or Hunold if we too are captured before we can aid them?"

"What *are* you doing?" I demanded.

"We have a fix on the source of the broadcast, or whatever it is. On top of the cliff to the east-northeast. But in the middle of the night we aren't going to get far climbing around these rocks hunting for it. I can tell you this much —it registers with too regular a pattern to be a human mind-send. If it is an installation, which we can believe, working on a telepath's level—then there should be someone in charge of it. Someone who probably knows this country a lot better than we do. But we have our range finder out now—"

"And something else," Harkon cut in crisply. "I loosed a snooper, set on the recording pattern, as soon as Lidj reported this. That will broadcast back a pick-up picture when it locates anything which is not just rock and brush."

"So—" Lidj spoke again. "Now we shall adjourn to the control cabin and see what the snooper can tell us."

The Patrol are noted for their use of sophisticated equipment. They have refinements which are far ahead of those on Free Trader ships. I had heard of snoopers, though I had never seen one in action before.

There was a flutter on the surface of the small screen set over the visa-plate of the *Lydis*—a rippling of lines. But that continued without change and my impatience grew. All that Lidj had said was unfortunately true. If I could not use mind-seek without provoking such instant retaliation as before, I had little chance of finding Maelen in that broken country, especially at night.

"Something coming in!" Harkon's voice broke through my dark imaginings.

Those fluttering lines on the screen were overlaid with a pattern. As we watched, the faint image sharpened into a definite scene. We looked into a dark space where an arching of rocks made a niche. And the niche was occupied. It was the face of the man or being who stood there which riveted my attention first. Human—or was he? His eyes were closed as if he slept—or concentrated. Then the whole of the scene registered. He was not in the open, but rather enclosed in a box which, except for the space before his face, was opaque. That box had been wedged upright, so he faced outward.

At his feet was a smaller box. But this was broken, badly battered, wires and jagged bits of metal showing through cracks in it.

Harkon spoke first. "I think we can see why the broadcast suddenly failed. That thing in front is an alpha-ten amplifier, or was before someone gave it a good bashing. It's meant to project and heighten com relays. But I never heard of it being used to amplify telepathic sends before."

"That man," Lidj said as if he could not quite believe what he saw. "Then he is a telepath and his mind-send was so amplified."

"A telepath to a degree hitherto unknown, I would say," Lukas replied. "There's something else—he may be human-oid, but he's not of Terran stock. Unless of a highly mutated strain."

"How do you know?" Harkon asked for all of us.

"Because he's plainly in stass-freeze. And in that state you don't broadcast; you are not even alive, as we reckon life."

He glanced at us as if he now expected some outburst of denial. But I, for one, knew Lukas was never given to wild and unfounded statements. If he thought that closed-eyed stranger was in stass-freeze, I would accept his diagnosis.

Harkon shook his head slowly. Not as if he were prepared to argue with Lukas, but as if he could not honestly accept what he was seeing.

"Well, if he is in stass-freeze, at least he's tight in that box. He did not get there on his own. Somebody put him there."

"How about the snooper—can it pick up any back trail from that?" Lidj gestured to the screen. "Show us who installed the esper and the amplifier?"

"We can see what a general life-force setting will do." Harkon studied the dial of his wrist com, made a delicate adjustment to it. The screen lost the picture with a flash and the fluttering returned.

"It isn't coming back," Harkon reported, "so the life-force search must be at work. But as to what it will pick up—"

"Getting something!" Korde leaned forward, half cutting off my view of the screen, so I pulled him back a little.

He was right. Once more there was a scene on the screen. We were looking into a much brighter section of country-side.

"The cache—they're looting the cache!" But we did not need that exclamation from Lidj.

There were excavation robos busy there. And they had broken through the plug we had thought the perfect pro-tection. Three—no, four—men stood a little to one side watching the work. Two were armed with blasters, one had a robo control board. But the fourth man—

I saw Lidj hunch farther toward the screen.

"I—don't—believe—it!" His denial was one we could have voiced as a chorus.

I knew Griss Sharvan; I had shared planet leave with him. He had been with me on Yiktor when first I had seen Maelen. It was utterly incredible that he should be standing there calmly watching the looting of our cargo. He was a Free Trader, born and bred to that life—and among us there were no traitors!

"He can only be mind-washed!" Lidj produced the one explanation we could accept. "If an esper of the power Krip met got at him, it's no wonder they could find the cache. They could pick its hiding place right out of his brain! And they must have Hunold, too. But what are they —jacks?" He asked that of Harkon, depending upon the authority of one who should know his lawbreakers to give him an answer.

"Jacks—with such equipment? They don't make such

elaborate efforts in their operations. I would think more likely a Guild job—"

"Thieves' Guild here?"

Lidj had a good right to his surprise. The Thieves' Guild was powerful, as everyone knew. But they did not operate on the far rim of the galaxy. Theirs was not the speculation of possible gains from raiding on frontier planets. Those small pickings were left to the jacks. The Guild planned bigger deals based on inner planets where wealth gathered, drawn in from those speculative ventures on the worlds the jacks plundered. If jacks had dealings with the Guild it was only when they fenced their take with the more powerful criminals. But they were very small operators compared with the members of that spider web which was, on some worlds, more powerful than the law. The Guild literally owned planets.

"Guild, or perhaps Guild-subsidized." Harkon held to his point stubbornly.

Which made our own position even more precarious, though it would also account for the sabotage and the elaborate plan which seemed to have been set up to enmesh the *Lydis*, both in space and here. The Guild had resources which even the Patrol could not guess. They were rumored to be ready to buy up, or acquire by other, more brutal means, new discoveries and inventions, so that they might keep ahead of their opponents. The boxed esper with the amplifier—yes, that could well be a Guild weapon. And the mining robos we saw at work here—

I thought at once of that cat mask on the cliff, of Maelen's assurance that other finds existed. Suppose some enterprising jack outfit, ambitious and far-seeing, had made the discovery that Sekhmet had such finds. With such a secret as their portion of the partnership, they could get Guild backing. At least to the extent of modern excavation equipment, plus such devices as the esper linkage for protection.

Then one of their men on Thoth could have picked up the news of our cargo. And they might have prepared to gather that in as a bonus. The Throne of Qur would be worth any effort. I could not help but believe that was the answer.

But what other devices could they have? That which sabotaged the *Lydis* we still do not understand. And the esper was something entirely new. Nor were the Free Traders backward in hearing about such things.

"Look out!"

I was startled out of my thoughts by Harkon's cry. We could still see the scene of the cargo cache. The robos had started to bring out what we had stored there. But it was not that action which the Patrol pilot had noted.

One of the guards had turned about, was pointing his blaster directly at our screen. A moment later that went black.

"Took out the snooper," Harkon commented.

"Now they know—first, that their esper is no longer controlling us; second, that we have learned of their activities in turn," Lidj said. "Do we now expect an attack in force?"

"What arms do you carry?" Harkon asked.

"No more than are allowed. We can break our seal on the ordnance compartment and get the rest of the blasters. That's the extent of it. A Trader depends on evasive action in space. And the *Lydis* does not set down on worlds where the weapons are much more sophisticated than on Thoth. We haven't broken that seal in years."

"And we don't know what they have—could be anything," Harkon commented. "I wonder who took out that amplifier. Might that man of yours be operating on his own—the one you did not see?"

But I was as certain as if I had witnessed the act. "Maelen did that."

"An animal—even a telepathic one—" Harkon began.

I eyed him coldly. "Maelen is not an animal. She is a Thassa, a Moon Singer of Yiktor." The odds were that he had not the slightest idea of what that meant, so I enlarged on that statement. "She is an alien, wearing animal form only for a time. It is a custom among her people." I was determined not to go farther into that. "She would be perfectly capable of tracing the esper interference and knocking out the amplifier."

But where was she now? Had she gone on to the cache to see what was happening there? I did not know how the jack guard had picked the snooper off so accurately. They were programmed to evade attack. He could have been just as quick to dispose of Maelen, had he sighted her. They had probably been planeted on Sekhmet long enough to know most of the native wildlife, so they would have recognized her even in animal form as something from off-world, and been suspicious. I could imagine plainly the whole sequence of such a discovery.

If only I dared mind-search! But even though the amplifier was not of use, I knew I could once more bring upon myself that force I had experienced earlier. Until the stass-

frozen man—or thing—was rendered harmless (if he could
be) I had no hope of tracking Maelen except by sight alone.
And in the dark of night that was impossible.

"We can just sit it out," Korde was saying when I again
paid attention. "Your ship"—he nodded to Harkon—"will
be back soon with Foss. We have power enough to warn
them once they come into braking orbit."

But Lidj was shaking his head. "Not good enough. The
jacks must have been watching us all along, even if we could
not detect them—they certainly possess a protective field
which blanks out even esper when they want, or Maelen
would have picked them up earlier. So they know about us
and that we are waiting for help. They could move fast
now—pack up and be off-world before we get reinforcements. After all, their base may be half this continent away,
hidden anywhere. We've got to keep on their tails if we can.
But it won't do any good to try another snooper. They will
be watching for that now."

"We haven't one anyway," Harkon commented dryly.
"For the rest, I would say you are right. There is also this—
if we stay in or around your ship, they may be able to pin us
down, blank out any com warning, hold us just as tightly
as they did before. I say, leave the ship with a guard and a
locked-up boarding ramp. The rest of us will take to the
country. It is rough enough to hide an army. We'll work our
way northeast, starting at the cache, and see if we can at
least locate the general direction of their base. They won't
be able to transport all they are pulling out of there without
making a number of trips. Also—that esper is still up there.
If we find him before they come to see what is wrong, we
may just be able to shut him off, or do whatever needs to be

done to hinder them in using him again. And what about this Maelen of yours—can you contact her, find out where she is?" He spoke directly to me.

"Not as long as that esper is broadcasting. You saw what happened when I tried that before. But I think she is near that cache. It may be that if I get close enough she can perhaps pick me up, though I can't be sure. She is far more powerful than I am."

"Good. That makes you our first choice for the scouting force." He certainly did not wait for volunteers. Not that I would not have been the first of those. But a Free Trader does not take kindly to any assumption of authority except from his own kind. And it was very apparent that Harkon considered himself without question to be the leader of any sortie we planned.

Lidj might have challenged him, but he did not. He went instead to break the seal on the arms locker. We took out the blasters, inserted fresh charges, slung on ammunition belts. E rations were in packets. And we had our thermo suits as protection against the chill.

In the end Korde and Aljec Lalfarns, a tubeman, stayed with the ship. Harkon's gunners from the flitter removed the charges from those crafts' defense to render them harmless and made ready to join us. It was still dark, though dawn could not now be too far away. We had a short rest and ate our last full ship's meal before we left.

It was decided we would try the more arduous climb up over the cliff, so we could find the esper and take action to insure he would not trouble us again. And climb we did, the blasters on their slings over our shoulders, weighing us back, making the climb more difficult, though the face of the stone was already rough enough. We had had to put aside our mittens in order to find handholes, and the chill of the rock bit deep, so that we must press on as quickly as we could before any numbing of our fingers could bring about disaster. I thought of Maelen's sharp-pointed claws and knew that this road must have been a fairly easy one for her. But her passing had left no traces.

We reached the top of the cliff, spread out in a single thin line as Harkon ordered. From this height we could see the lights at the location of the cache. The workers there made no effort to hide their presence. And, having been alerted by the snooper, they could already be preparing a warm welcome.

Our advance had been very short when my wrist com buzzed. "To the right," clicked the signal which brought me in that direction, picking my way more by feel than sight.

Thus we gathered at the niche we had seen from the snooper. The smashed amplifier had not been moved. It was apparent that those who had installed it there either had not arrived to check on it, or had abandoned it. I stepped closer, flinched. For the first time in my life I experienced mind-send not only in my brain, but as an invisible but potent force against my body.

"Don't go directly in front of it!" I said sharply.

At my warning Harkon edged in from one side, I from the other. There was no sign of life on that face. It was humanoid, yet it had an alien cast. I might have been look-ing at a dead man, in fact I would have said so, had I not felt that strong current of send. The Patrolman stepped back, yielding his place to Lukas. Now the medic put out his unmittened hand and moved his fingers, held an inch or so away from the surface of that case, as if he were smoothing it up and down.

"Stass-freeze to a high degree," he reported. "Higher than I know of in general use." He unsealed the front of his jacket, drew out a life-force detect, and held that at the level of the sleeper's chest, though we could not see the body through that opaque opening.

In the very dim light radiated by the box I saw the incredulous expression on Lukas's face. With a sharp jerk he brought the detect up level with the head, took a second reading, returned to heart level for another examination. Then he edged back.

"What about it?" Harkon asked. "How deep in stass is he?"

"Too deep—he's dead!"

"But he can't be!" I stared at the set face of the box's occupant. "The dead don't mind-send!"

"Maybe he doesn't know that!" Lukas gave a queer sound, almost a laugh. Then his voice steadied as he added, "He's not only dead, but so long dead the force reading went clear out of reckoning. Think about that for a moment."

Chapter 9

KRIP VORLUND

I still could not really believe that. A mind-send from a dead man—impossible! And I said so. But Lukas waved his detect and swore that it was working properly, as he proved by trying it on me and pointing to the perfectly normal reading. We had to accept that a dead body, linked to an amplifier, had managed to keep us in thrall until the machine had been smashed; that esper power, strong enough to upset anyone human (I could hope Maelen was beyond its control) who tried to use a like talent in its vicinity, was issuing from a dead man.

But the cache was still being looted. We dared not spend too long a time with this mystery when action was demanded elsewhere. The damaged amplifier was speedily disposed of, but we could not unwedge that box. So we left the strange sleeper there, still broadcasting, as he had— for how long? Though I was sure not from the same site.

The way over the cliffs was much shorter than the

ground-level trail. We crept up, following all the precautions of those invading enemy territory, until we could look
down at the cache. There the robos had emptied our hiding
place. The glittering Throne stood in a blaze of harsh glory
amid the boxes and bundles.

A flitter, perhaps double the size of our own, had
grounded, was being loaded with the smaller pieces. The
three jacks we had seen via snooper were studying the
Throne. It was plain to see that that was not going to fit
into the flyer, and its transportation must present a problem.

Save for those three there appeared to be no one else
below. Sharvan had disappeared. But at the moment my
own concern was for Maelen. If she had come here, was she
hiding somewhere among these rocks, spying as we were?
Dared I try mind-send again?

There was no other way of finding her in this rough
terrain. Though one of Sekhmet's cloudy dawns was at
hand and visibility was better than it had been when we
had begun this trek. I made my choice for mind-seek, ready
to withdraw that instantly if I so much as brushed the edge
of any deadly broadcast. But this time I met none. So
heartened, I fastened upon a mind-picture of Maelen and
began my quest in earnest.

But I did not even meet with the betraying signal of a
mind-block. She was not on the heights where we lay in
hiding. Down in the valley near the cache then? Very
cautiously I began to probe below, fearing to trigger some
such response as I had before. They might well have a
second sleeper at the scene of action as a cover.

I met nothing, and that in itself was kind of a shock.
For all three of those I could see conferring about the

Throne did not register at all. They were mind-shielded
with a complete barrier against any probe. Perhaps because
of the fact that they dealt with the sleeper, and only thus
could they venture to use him. So there was nothing to be
learned from them either. Nor did Maelen's answer come
from the valley.

Having made sure of that, I began to extend my search—
choosing south, the way from which we had come when we
had first discovered this place. And, as my send crept on
and on, I picked up the faintest quiver of an answer!

"Where—where?" I put full force into that.

"—here—" Very faint, very far away. "—aid—here—"

There could be no mistaking the urgency of her plea.
But the low volume of the send was an even greater spur to
action. That Maelen was in dire trouble, I had no doubt
at all. And the choice I must make now was equally plain.
The cargo had brought us here; it was the responsibility of
the *Lydis*'s crew. We were eight men against an unknown
number.

And there was Maelen—lost—calling for my aid.

The decision as partly dictated by my Thassa body, of
that I am now sure. Just as I had once feared that Jorth
the barsk was stronger than Krip Vorlund the man, so now
Maquad of the Thassa—or that small residue of him which
was a part of me—changed my life. Thassa to Thassa—I
could not hold out against that call. But neither would my
other heritage allow me to go without telling my own kind
that I must.

Chance had brought me closest to Lidj. I crawled now
until I could set hand on his shoulder. He jerked at my

touch, turned to look at me. Dusky as this cloud-shrouded
day was, we could see each other clearly.

"Maelen is in trouble. She is calling me for aid," I told
him in a whisper which I meant to carry no farther than
this spot.

He said nothing, nor did any expression cross his face.
I do not know what I expected, but that long, level look
was one I had to force myself to meet. Though I waited, he
continued silent. Then he turned away to gaze into the
valley. I was chilled, cold, as if the thermo jacket had been
ripped from my body, leaving my shoulders bare to the
winds.

Yet I could not bite back my words; there was that in me
which held me to my choice. I turned and crawled. Not
only from the side of the cargomaster, but from that whole
length of cliff where the others crouched waiting for
Harkon's signal to attack, if that was the order he would
give.

Now I had to force from me all thought of those of the
Lydis. I must concentrate wholly on that thread, so thin, so
far-stretched, which tied me to Maelen. And a thin, far-
stretched one it was, so tenuous I feared it would be
severed and I would have no guide at all.

It brought me down from the cliffs. And I could not mistake landmarks I had memorized. This was the way to the
cat mask. I reached a point from which I ought to be able
to see that pale and ghostly vestige of ancient carving. But
this morning the light, perhaps the lack of sand to cling
in the right places, did not aid me. I could trace nothing
but the hollow which was its mouth.

And Maelen's desperate call led me there. I wriggled forward on my belly, expecting she must lie there in the shadows. But the pocket was empty! Only her call continued—from beyond the wall!

With my mittened hands I pushed and beat against the blocks, certain that there must be some concealed door, that one or another of them would fall or turn to provide me with an opening. How else could Maelen have entered?

But the blocks were as firmly joined as if they had been set in place but weeks before.

"Maelen!" I lay there, my hands resting against the wall. "Maelen, where are you?"

"Krip—aid—aid—"

Faint, far away, a cry fast fading into nothingness. And the fear which had been riding me since first I picked up her send now struck deep into me. I was certain that if I could not find a way to her soon there would be no reason to go at all. Maelen would be gone for all time.

I had but one key left to use. And by using it I might throw away a means for my own defense. But again I had no choice. I edged back, out of the mouth of that cleft.

I lay flat outside, sighting inward with the blaster. Then I dropped my head to my bent arm, veiling my eyes against the brilliance of the blast I loosed as I fired.

Scorching heat beat back against me, though the worst was absorbed by my thermo clothing. I smelled the crisping of my mittens, felt a searing lick across the edge of my cheek. Still I held fast, giving that inner wall top power. What effect it would have on the blocks I could not tell; I could only hope.

When I had used all that charge I had yet to wait, not

daring at once to crawl back within that cramped space
until it had a little time to lose some of the heat. But
neither could I wait too long.

At last impatience won, and I was startled at what I
found. Those blocks, which to the touch had had a likeness
to the native rock of the cliff wall, were gone—as cleanly
as if they had only been counterfeits of stone. Thus I was
able to enter the passage beyond.

Not that that was much larger. The cleft, or tunnel, or
whatever it was, ran straight as a bore, with just enough
room to wriggle. As I advanced I liked the situation less
and less. Had I even been able to rise to my hands and
knees, it would have given me a measure of relief. As it
was, I had to edge on with a maximum of effort in a mini-
mum of space.

Also, the farther I went, the less I liked the idea of perhaps coming up against a dead end and having to work my
way out backward. In fact, so disturbing did I find that
thought that I had to banish it as quickly as I could by
holding to my mental picture of Maelen.

That journey seemed endless, but it was not. I used the
blaster, now empty of charge, as a sounding rod, pushing
it ahead of me through the dark, so feeling for any ob-
struction or fault which might cause trouble. And that did
at last strike a solid surface.

I probed with the blaster in exploration, and it seemed
that the passage was firmly plugged ahead. But I must make
sure, so I squirmed on until my hand came against that
surface. It did fill the space, and yet into my face blew a
puff of air. Though hitherto I had not even wondered why
I had been able to breathe in this tightly confined space.

As I slipped my hands back and forth, my fingers discovered a hole, through which flowed a distinct current of air. Hooking one hand to that, I strove to dislodge the whole plug. My effort moved it, though I found I must push instead of pull. It swung away from me and I shouldered through.

So I came not only to a much larger space, but to one with dim lighting. Or perhaps it was dim only in comparison with the outer world. To my eyes, used now to total dark, it seemed bright.

The hole of my entrance was some distance above the floor of this other space. I entered in an awkward scramble, half falling to the lower level. It was so good to stand erect again.

This chamber was square. And the light came through a series of long, narrow cuts set vertically in the wall to my left. Save for those, there appeared to be no other opening, certainly no door.

When I advanced to the light, I discovered a grating in the floor against the wall, wide enough for an exit if there were some manner of raising the grating itself. Just now I was more intent on looking through one of the slits.

It was necessary to squeeze very close to that narrow opening. Even then the area of vision was much curtailed. But I was looking down into a room or hall which was of such large proportions I could view only a fraction of it. The light came from the tops of a series of standing pillars or cases. And a moment's inspection of the nearest, though I must do that from some distance above, suggested something familiar. By almost grinding my face against the frame of the slit, I made a guess. These had a close resem-

blance to the box which had held that dead man above
the valley. I was looking into a place for beings in stass-
freeze!

"Maelen?"

Nothing moved below among the pillar-boxes. And—I
had no answer to my call. I went on my knees, shed my
charred mittens so I could lock fingers in the grating. And
I had to exert all the strength I could summon before that
gave, grudgingly. However, I was able to raise it. How I
longed for what I did not have—a torch, for there was only
dark below once more.

Lying flat, I tried to gauge what did lie below by letting
the blaster dangle from its carrying strap. Thus I discovered
what appeared to be a narrow shaft, its floor not too far
below. And I dared to drop to that. Once down, I explored
the wall which faced the sleepers' hall and was able to trace
a line. Pushing outward brought no results. It was when my
hands slipped across the surface of that stubborn barrier
that it moved to one side and I was able to force it open
a crack. Then the barrel of the blaster inserted there gave
me leverage enough to force it the rest of the way.

How large that hall was I could not guess. It appeared to
stretch endlessly both right and left. And there was such a
sameness to those lines of boxes one could not find any
guide.

"Maelen?"

I fell back against the very door I had just forced open.
As it had happened before, my mind-seek brought such an
answer as nearly struck me down. This response was no
concentrated beam, but still it was a daunting blast, filling
my mind painfully. So I crouched there, my hands raised

to my ears in an involuntary response as if to shut out thundering shouts.

It was a torment, worse than any physical pain. A warning that here I dared not use the only way I had of tracing her whom I sought. I would have to blunder along, depending on the whim of fortune.

Shutting out mind-seek, I staggered forward in a wavering way between the boxes in the row directly before me. Now and then I paused to study the faces of those sleepers. There was a sameness about those. They might all have come from some uniform mold, as there appeared to be no distinguishing marks to make one case differ from the next. Then I became a little less dazed by that mental bolt which had struck me and noted that there was a change in the patterning of color sparks about the frame of each box.

I counted at first, but after I reached fifty, I decided there was no need for that. Beyond the rows where I walked now were more and more and more. It might be that the entire army of some forgotten conqueror was here laid up in stass-freeze. I laughed then, thinking what an excellent way to preserve troops between one war and the next, assuring a goodly supply of manpower with no interregnum living expenses.

Such a find as this had never been made before. In fact the treasure discoveries on Thoth had had no conjunction with the remains of bodies, a puzzle for the archaeologists, since it had previously been believed that such furnishings were placed with rulers as grave goods. So—was this the cemetery of those who had left their treasures on Thoth? But why, then, cross space to bury their dead on another world?

And if they were dead, why were their bodies in stass-freeze? It was a condition known to my own kind in the past, used for two purposes. In the very early days of space travel it had been the only way to transport travelers during long voyages which might last for centuries of planet time. Secondly, it was the one hope for the seriously ill, who could rest thus until some future medical discovery could cure them.

Nations, peoples, even species did entomb their dead, following beliefs that at the will of their gods, or at some signal, these would rise whole and alive again. Was this so profound a belief here that they had used stass-freeze to preserve their dead?

I could accept such preservation, but I could not accept the fact that, although dead, they apparently still used their esper powers. My mind shied away from the horror that a live mind could be imprisoned in a dead body.

There was an end at last to the hall. In the faint light of the boxes I could now see another wall, and in that an arch-way framing a wide door. A closed door. But I was so filled with a loathing of that place that I halted, fumbled for another charge for the blaster, determined to burn my way out if I found that portal barred to my exit.

However, at my urging it rolled aside into the wall. I looked into a passageway. It was lighted, though by what means I could not see, save that the walls themselves ap-peared to give off a gray luminosity. With the blaster ready I went along.

There were doors in this corridor, each tightly closed, each bearing on its surface a series of symbols which had no meaning for me. And where in all this maze could I

find Maelen? Since my sharp lesson in the hall of the
sleepers, I dared not risk another call. There was no help
but to look within each of the rooms I passed.

The first door opened on a small chamber holding but
two sleepers. But there were also chests ranged about its
walls. However, I did not wait to explore those. Another
room—three sleepers—more storage containers. Room
three—two sleepers again—more chests.

I was at the end of the hall and here the way branched
right and left. I chose the right. The hall was still lighted
and it ran straight, without any break. How many miles
did this burrowing run? I wondered. It might be that
Sekhmet was half honeycombed with these tunnelings.
What a find! And if those chests and boxes I had seen in
the smaller rooms contained such treasures as had been
found on Thoth—then indeed the jacks had uncovered a
mine which the Guild would not disdain to work. But why
had they jeopardized their operation by sabotaging the
Lydis? They could have worked here for years and never
been discovered, had we not been forced down and they
overplayed their hand by the attack on us. Was it a matter
of being over-greedy?

The corridor I now followed began to narrow; soon it
was passage for one only. There—I paused, my head up as
I sniffed. Some untrackable system of ventilation had supplied all these ways. But this was something different—it
was an odor I recognized. Somewhere not too far away
cyro leaves had been recently burned. There were other
faint scents also—food—cooked food—but the cyro overlaid most of that so strongly I could identify little else.

Cyro is mildly intoxicating, but it is also used as a counter

to both body fatigue and some nervous depressions. As a
Free Trader I was and am conditioned against certain drugs.
By the very nature of our lives we must keep ourselves alert
and with top powers of reaction. Just as we are conditioned
against a planetside interest in intoxicants of any type,
gambling, women not of our kind, so we know the drugs
which can spell danger by a clouding of mind, a slowing of
body. So well are we armored against such that the use of
any can make us violently ill.

Now I felt myself swallowing, fighting the nausea that
smell induced in me. But such an odor could mean nothing
less than that somewhere ahead were, or had been, others
than the sleepers. After such a warning my progress was
doubly cautious.

The hall ended in a blank wall, but then I saw an opening
to my right, framing a brighter glow some distance ahead.
And so I came out on a low-walled balcony overhanging
another large chamber. This in turn was partly open to the
sky. And beyond, in that daylight, I caught a glimpse of a
spacer's fins, as if one side of this cavern opened on a landing field.

There was no way down from the balcony. But from this
perch I had a good view of all which lay below. And there
was plenty to see. To one side was heaped a pile of such
chests and boxes as had been in the rooms. Many of them
had shattered lids as if they had been forced. And not too
far away two servo robos were fastening up a shipping crate.

Off to the right was a plasta-bubble, the kind of living
quarters used by explorers as a base camp. This was sealed.
But two men sat on upturned boxes outside it. One was
speaking into a wrist recorder. The other held a robo con-

trol board on his knee as he watched the two busy at the crate. There was no one else in sight.

I tried to gauge the ship's size from what I could see of its fins, and decided it must be at least equal to the *Lydis*, perhaps larger. But there was no doubting that I witnessed a well-established and full-sized operation, and that it had been going on for some time.

The last thing I wanted to do was attract their attention. But Maelen—had she wandered in here, to be caught in some trap? Indecision held me fast. Dare I mind-call? There were no sleepers visible. But that did not mean that the jacks might not be using one as a defense or a warning.

I was still hesitating when a man came in from outside. Griss Sharvan!

Griss—I still could not accept that he was a part of this, or that he had of his own free will gone over to the enemy. I had known him far too long, and he was a Free Trader. Yet he moved freely, gave no sign of being a prisoner.

He joined the two by the bubble. The one recording got to his feet hurriedly, as did his companion. They gave the response of underlings in the presence of a leader. What— what had happened to Griss?

Suddenly his attention turned from them. His head came up, he stared straight up—at me! I fell behind the low wall edging the balcony. His actions had been those of a man alerted to danger, one who knows just where to look.

I began to crawl back to the passage which had brought me here. Only I never reached it. For what struck me then was something I had never experienced before, in spite of my many encounters with different kinds of esper power.

The command of my own body was taken from me. It was as if my mind was imprisoned in a robo which was obeying commands broadcast by a board. I got to my feet, turned around, and marched back into the sight of the three below, all of whom now watched me.

Griss raised his hand, pointed a forefinger at me. To my complete amazement I was raised from the stone under my boots, lifted above the wall, carried out and down, all as if I had antigrav on me. Nor could I struggle against that compelling force which held me captive.

That energy deposited me, still on my feet, on the floor of the cavern. I stood there, a prisoner, as the two who had been checking cargo advanced on me. Griss remained where he was, that pointing finger aimed at my head, as if his flesh and bone had become a tangler.

The man who still held the robo control reached out his other hand and snatched the blaster from my hold. Even then my hands did not change position, but remained as if I still gripped barrel and butt with them. But the other jack brought out a real tangler, spinning its web of restraint around me. When he was done, Griss's hand dropped and that compulsion was gone, though now I had no chance at freedom. They had left my legs unbound, and the jack with the tangler caught my shoulder and gave me a vicious shove toward Griss.

Chapter 10

KRIP VORLUND

Only it was not Griss Sharvan who stood there. Though he—it—wore Griss's body as one might wear a thermo suit. The minute those eyes met mine, I knew. Nor did that knowledge come as too great a shock, since my own experiences had taught me such shifts were possible.

However, this was no shift for the sake of knowledge, nor for the preservation of life, such as the Thassa practiced. The personality which had taken over Griss was alien to our kind as the Thassa could never be. I had a swift mental picture of a terrifying creature—a thing with a reasonably humanoid body but a head evilly reptilian, a mixture which repelled.

Only for an instant did I hold that mental image; then it was gone. But with its disappearance there was also a flash of incredulous surprise, not on my part, but from the alien. As if he—it—was astounded that I had been able to pick up that image at all, as its true nature was so well concealed it never revealed itself.

"Greeting, Krip." Griss's voice. But I knew well that those slow, toneless words carried another's thoughts. I did not attempt any mental scanning, being warned by instinct that such would be the most dangerous thing I could do. "How many are with you?"

He held his head a little to one side, giving the impression of listening. A moment later he smiled.

"So you are alone, Krip? Now that was very foolish of you. Not that the whole crew could take us. But if they had been so obliging as to come it would have saved us much trouble. However, one more is a good beginning."

His eyes searched mine, but I had been warned enough to draw on the full resources of my talent, erect a mind-shield. Against that I could feel his probing, but surprisingly, he did not try to force it. I feared, guessed, that had he wanted to, he could easily have stripped me of any defenses, taken over my mind to learn all I had been trying to hide from him. This was a master esper, such as perhaps were the Old Ones among the Thassa, far beyond my own talent.

"A beginning," he repeated. Then he raised his hand in an arrogant gesture, crooking his finger to beckon me. "Come!"

I had not the slightest hope of disobeying that order. As before, I walked helplessly after him across the cavelike chamber. Never once did he turn his head to see whether or no I was behind, but wove a path in and out among the boxes.

So we came to another door and into a passage beyond. The light faded once again to that gray gloom which I had seen above, and the passage made several turns. Along its walls were open doors, but all the rooms were empty.

That this creature wearing Griss's body meant me no good was evident. I believed that my only defense against dire and instant peril was to dampen all esper talent, to depend only on the five senses of my body. But those I used as best I could to give me some idea of the territory through which we passed.

There were traces of odors from the cyro, but they were soon gone, leaving only an indefinable scent I could not name. Sight gave me the passage and the empty rooms along it. Sound—there was the faint rasp of two pairs of space boots against the stone floor, the fainter pulsing of my own breathing—nothing else.

And where was Maelen? A prisoner perhaps in the bubble? As quickly as I thought of her I thrust that thought again from my conscious mind. If she had not been discovered, I must not betray her.

My captor turned his head to glance back at me. And I shivered. He was laughing silently, his whole body quivering in a horrible travesty of the honest mirth my species knew. And his face was a mask of unholy and frightening joy—worse than any rictus born of torture or wrath.

Yet he made no effort to speak, either orally or by mind-touch. And I did not know whether that made his unseemly laughter, that silent gloating laughter, better or worse—probably the latter. Still laughing, he turned from the hallway into one of those rooms, and, still helplessly in thrall, I followed.

The gray light of the corridor held here, but the room was empty. My captor stepped briskly to the left-hand wall. Once more he put out his hand, pointing a finger even as he had used it to make me prisoner. If he did not touch the

surface of the stone, he came very close to it. So he began
to trace a series of complicated lines. But as his finger
moved there glowed on the wall a glistening thread, weaving in and out.

I knew that it was a symbol. We have devices such as
persona locks which can be opened only by the body heat
and thumb pattern of the one setting them. It could be that
what I now saw was a very sophisticated development of
such a safeguard, coming to life when will alone was focused
on it.

He drew a design of sharp angles, of lines which to my
eyes not only were distorted, but bothered me to look upon,
as if they followed rules so alien that the human eye found
them disturbing. Yet I could not look away.

Finally the alien seemed satisfied with the complicated
pattern of line-cross-line, line-upon-line. Now his pointing
finger indicated the very heart of the drawing. So he might
have opened a well-concealed lock.

Sound answered, a grating—a protest, as if too long a
time had passed since certain mechanisms had been acti-
vated. The wall split, a straight-edged crack down through
the center of the design. One portion moved to each side
to form a narrow doorway. Without hesitation he stepped
within, and again I was drawn on.

There was no light here, and what sifted in from the
chamber behind was sharply cut off as that crack closed.
Where we stood now, in another chamber or a corridor, I
had no idea. But that pressure kept me walking ahead. By
the faint sounds, I deduced that he whom I trailed went as
confidently as if he traveled a lighted and well-known road.

I fought an imagination which was only too ready to

picture for me all which might lie underfoot, on either side, even overhead. There was no way of escape. And I had best save my energy, hold my control, for a time when I might have some small chance against that which walked in Griss Sharvan's body.

To travel in utter darkness, and by another's will, distorts time. Minutes might have been stretching, or else they were less—I had no way of telling. It seemed to me that we went so for a long time, yet it may not have been that at all.

Then—light!

I closed my eyes against what seemed to be a wild burst of eye-hurting color. Blinked, closed, opened—

The chamber in which we stood was four-sided with walls which sloped inward, to meet at an apex well over our heads. And those walls were also transparent, so we might have been inside a pyramid-shaped room of crystal.

Through the transparent walls we looked into four rooms. And each had its occupant, an unmoving, unbreathing occupant, who yet seemed no statue but a living creature, or once-living creature, frozen into complete immobility.

I say "creature," for while these preserved beings beyond the walls were humanoid to at least the ninth degree outwardly, I had, as I looked upon them, the same sensation of an indweller wholly alien. For three I had that sensation. For the fourth—I gazed the longest at him—and knew, shocked into applying mind-probe to learn the truth.

Griss—that was Griss! As tightly bound within that body as I now was in the tangler's cords. He was only dimly conscious of what had happened to him, but enough so that

he was living in an endless nightmare. And how long his
reason could so endure—

I wrenched my eyes away, fearing to draw the crushing
burden of his fear just when I needed a clear mind. Such
would be no aid to him. Instead I made myself examine
more closely the other three who waited there.

The rooms themselves were elaborately furnished, the
furniture carven, inlaid with gems. Two had narrow beds,
the supporting posts of which were the bodies of strange
animals or birds; two, chairs which bore a small likeness to
the Throne of Qur. Tables with small boxes; chests.

Then—the inhabitants. Whereas the bodies I had seen in
the freeze boxes had been bare, these all wore helmets or
crowns. They also possessed eyelashes and eyebrows. Each
crown differed also, representing grotesque creatures. I shot
another quick glance at that body now holding Griss's
identity.

The crown it wore was a brown-yellow in the form of a
wide-jawed saurian thing which was akin to the head I had
seen in the mental image I had picked up earlier. It sat in
a chair, but the one behind the next wall reclined on the
narrow bed, head and shoulders supported by a rest of
decorated material. The third was seated again. The crown
of the second was a bird, and that of the third a sharp-
muzzled, prick-eared animal.

But the fourth of that company was a woman! None of
those behind the walls were clothed except for their crowns.
And their bodies were flawless, akin to the ideal of beauty
held by my species. The woman was such perfection as I
had never dreamed could exist in the flesh. From beneath

her diadem flowed hair to clothe her almost to her knees. That hair was of a red so deep and dark as to seem nearly black. Her crown was not as massive as those which seemed to weigh down her companions, but rather a band from which sprang a series of upstanding but uneven and unmatched filaments. Then I saw more clearly that each of these bore on its tip a small head like that mask of the cliff face. And each of those heads was equipped with gem eyes.

I gasped. When I had looked directly at the woman those cats' heads of her crown had begun to move, to turn, to rise, until they were all stiffly upstanding, pointing outward as if their jewel eyes were looking back at me in alert measurement.

But her own eyes stared beyond me as if I were so far outside her inner world that I had no existence for her.

A hand on my shoulder brought me around—to face the seated alien with the animal crown. And in my ears, Griss's voice:

"Attend, you! A great honor for this puny body of yours. It shall be worn by—" If he had meant to utter some name, he did not. And I think he cut short his words because of caution.

There is a belief, found mainly among primitive peoples, that to tell another one's true name puts one at his mercy. But that such a superstition would persist among aliens with manifestly so high a level of advancement I could not altogether believe.

However, that he intended now to force such an exchange as there had been for Griss, I had no doubts at all.

And I was as afraid as I never remembered being before in my entire life.

He caught my head from behind, held it in a vise grip, so that I had to look eye to eye with that one behind the wall. There was no fighting for freedom. Not physically. But still I could fight, I would! And I drew upon all the reserves of esper I had, all my sense of being who and what I was. I was only just quick enough to meet the attack.

It was not the harsh blanketing which had served as the knockout blow I had met in the ship valley, but rather a pointed thrust, delivered with arrogant self-confidence. And I was able to brace against it without bringing all my own power to bear.

Though I did not then catch any surprise, there was a sudden cut-off of pressure. As if he of the animal crown retreated, puzzled by resistance where he had thought to find none at all, retreated to consider what he might actually be facing. While I, given that very short respite, braced myself to await what I was sure would be a much stronger and tougher attack.

It came. I was no longer aware of anything outside, only of inner tumult, where some small core of my personality was beaten by smothering wave after wave of will; trying to breach my last defense and take that inner me captive. But —I held, and knew the crowned one's astonishment at such holding. Shock after shock against my will, still I was not engulfed, lost, borne away. Then I felt that other's growing rage, uncertainty. And I was sure that those waves of pressure were not so strong, that they were ebbing faster and farther as a tide might withdraw from a shore cliff which was mercilessly beaten by the sea but which still stood.

Awareness of the room returned. My head, still in that hold, was up, eye to eye with him beyond the wall. His face was as expressionless as it had ever been. Yet those features seemed contorted, hideous with a rage born of frustration.

"He will not do!" It was almost a scream within my head, bringing pain with the raw emotion with which it struck. "Take him hence! He is a danger!"

My captor jerked me around. Griss's face before me, but the expression was not his, an ugly, raw menace the real Griss had never shown. I thought that he might well burn me down. Yet it seemed he might have some other use for me, for he did not reach for the blaster at his belt but rather sent me sprawling forward, so that I skidded up against the crystal surface of the wall behind which lay the woman, if woman she had ever been.

The cat-headed filaments of her crown quivered, dipped, their eyes glinting avidly as they watched me. I slid to my knees as if I were offering some homage to an unresponsive queen. But she stared unseeingly above my head.

The alien pulled me up, sent me on, with another push, toward the narrow slit of a doorway near one corner of the room. Then I was for the second time in the full darkness of that passage, this time ahead of my captor.

Nor was I to make the full return journey; for we were not far along that tunnel, in a dark so thick one could almost feel it, before I was again propelled to the right. I did not strike against any wall there, but kept on, brushing one of my shoulders against a smooth surface.

"I do not know what you are, Krip Vorlund," Griss's

voice rang out of the dark. " 'Thassa,' says that poor fool
whose seeming I wear. It would appear that you are a different breed, with some armor against our will. But this is no
time for the solving of riddles. If you survive you may give
us an entertaining puzzle at a later hour. *If* you survive!"

Painfully alert to whatever guides I could use in this dark,
I thought his voice sounded fainter, as if he no longer
stood close by. Then there was only the dark and the
silence, which in its way was as overpowering as the blackness blinding me. No compulsion to follow; I was as free as
if a cord had been cut. But my arms were still tightly
bound to my sides by the constriction of tangle cords.

I listened, trying even to breathe as lightly as I could so
that would not hide any possible sound. Nothing—nothing
but the horrible weight of the smothering dark. Slowly I
took one step and then another from the wall, which was
my only point of reference. Two more—three steps—and I
came up against another wall. If I had only had the use of
my hands, it would have been a small relief, but that was
denied me.

Exploration, so hindered, told me at last that the narrow
space in which I stood must be the end of another corridor.
I found I could not return the way we had come—if my
sense of direction had not altogether failed me—for that
had been cut off, though I had not heard the closing of any
door. There were left only the three walls, with the fourth
side open. Leading perhaps to a multitude of possible
disasters. But these I must chance blindly.

It was slow progress, that blind creeping, my right
shoulder brushing ever against the wall, since I had to have
some reference. I found no door, no other opening, always

the same smooth surface against which my thermo jacket brushed with a soft rustling. And it went on and on—

I was tired—more, I was hungry, and thirst made my mouth and throat as dry as the ashy sand of the valley. To know that I carried at my own belt the means of alleviating all my miseries made it doubly hard. There was no fighting the grip of the tangle bond. To do so would lead to greater and more dangerous constriction. Twice I slipped to the floor of the passage. It was so narrow I had to hunch up with bent knees to rest, for the toes of my boots grated against the other wall. But then to get up again required such effort that the last time I did so, I thought I must keep on my feet and going, with a thin hope of survival. For if I went down again it could well be I would never have the strength to rise.

On and on—this was like one of those nightmares in which one is forced to wade through some muck which hinders each step, and yet behind comes a hunter relentlessly in chase. I knew my hunter—my own weakness.

Action held much of a dreamlike quality for me now. The four crowned ones—Griss Sharvan who was not Griss. Maelen—

Maelen! She had receded from my mind during that ordeal in the crystal room. Maelen! When I tried to see my mind-picture of her she flowed into someone else. Maelen— her long red hair, her— *Red* hair! No, Maelen had the silver hair of the Thassa, like that now close-cropped on my own skull. RED HAIR—the woman of the cat crown! I flinched. Could it be that some of that compulsion which had been loosed against me back there was still working on me?

Maelen. Laboriously I built my mental picture of her in

the Thassa body. And despairingly, not believing I would ever again have any reply from her, I sent out a mind-call.

"Krip! Oh, Krip!"

Sharp, clear, as if shouted aloud in joy because, after long searching, we had come face to face. I could not believe it even though I heard.

"Maelen?" If thought-send could whisper, then mine did.

"Krip, where are you? Come—oh, come—"

Clear; I had not been mistaken, misled. She was here, and close, or that call would not be so loud. I pulled myself together, made answer quickly as I could:

"I do not know where I am, except in a very dark and narrow passage."

"Wait—say my name, Krip. Give me a direction!"

I obeyed, making of her name a kind of mind-chant, knowing that here perhaps there was power in a name. For upon such a point of identity could a mind-send firmly anchor.

"I think that I have it. Come on—straight ahead, Krip."

I needed no more urging; my shuffle quickened. Though I still had to go with my shoulder along the wall, since I could not bear to lose that guide in the dark. It was good that I kept it so, for there was another sudden transition from the dark to light, enough to blind me temporarily, so I leaned against the wall with my eyes closed.

"Krip!"

So loud she could be there before me!

I opened my eyes. She was. Her black fur was grayed, matted with dust. She wavered from side to side as if she could hardly keep her feet. There was a blotch of dried blood along one side of her head. But she was alive.

I slipped down by the wall, edging out on my knees to bring me closer to her. But she had dropped to the floor as if no reserve of strength remained in her. Forgetting, I fought my bonds, then gasped as the resulting constriction punished me.

"Maelen!"

She lay, her head on her paws, flattened to the stone, much as she had lain on her bunk in the *Lydis*. But now her eyes were fast closed. It was as if the effort of guiding me to her had drained her last strength.

Food, water—by the look of her, her need for those was greater than my own. Yet I could not help her, not unless she first freed me. And I did not know if she could.

"Maelen, at my belt—the cutter—"

One of those tools which were the ever-present equipment of an adventurer on an unknown world.

Her eyes opened, looked to me. Slowly she raised her head, as if to do so was painful, or so fatiguing she could hardly manage it. She could not regain her feet, and she whimpered as she wriggled on her belly to my side.

Bracing herself against my body, she brought her head higher; her dust-caked muzzle rubbed my side as she nosed against my belt. While she had once been so graceful of body, she was now clumsy and awkward, taking a long time to free the cutter from its loop, though I turned and twisted to give her all the aid I could.

The tool lay in the dust for a long time (or so it seemed to me) before she bent her head to mouth its butt, bring it up to rest against the lowest loop of the tangle bond. Twice the cutter slid away to thud to the stone before she could bite down on the spring releasing its energy. My frustration

at having to watch her efforts and not be able to help made
me ill.

But she kept to it stubbornly and finally she made it.
The energy blade snipped into the thick round of the
tangle well enough so that my own struggles parted it.
Once broken, after the way of such, it shriveled away and I
was free, though my arms were numb and I found it difficult to lift them. A return of circulation was painful, but I
could grope for the rations in my supply bag. And I had
those at hand as I pulled Maelen's body closer, supported
her head against me, trickling water into her parched, dust-
rimmed mouth.

She swallowed once, again. I put aside the water container, licking my own lips, to unscrew an E-ration tube,
squirt the semiliquid contents into her mouth. So I fed
her half of that restorative nutriment before I slaked my
own thirst, fed my hunger-racked body.

For the first time, sitting there, holding the tube to my
mouth, Maelen resting against my knee, I really looked
about me. This was another of those pyramid-shaped
chambers, though it did not rise to a point but was sliced
off midway up with a square ceiling much smaller than the
floor area.

Nor were these walls crystal, but rock. The ledge where
we sat was about halfway between roof and floor. I turned
my head to see the doorway through which I had come.
But there was nothing—nothing at all! I remembered that
quick transition from dark to light, as if I had pushed
through a curtain.

There was a very steep stair midway along the ledge,
descending to the floor. And that floor supported a series of

blocks, some tall, others shorter, in uneven heights. Cresting each of these was a ball of some opaque substance which was not stone. And in the inner heart of each ball was a faint glimmer of light.

The balls were colored—red, blue, green, yellow, then violet, orange, paler shades, those closest to the walls the palest hues of all, deepening as one approached the core. The center one there was very dark indeed, almost black.

On the surfaces of the brighter and lighter-colored ones were etched patterns. And as I studied them I recognized some—there was a reptilian head resembling the crown of the body that now imprisoned Griss; I saw the animal one, the bird one, and, farthest away, a cat mask. But the meaning of this display or its use I could not guess. I leaned back against the wall; Maelen lay unmoving. I thought that she slept now and I had no desire to trouble her rest.

Rest—I needed that also. I shut my eyes to the dull light. Undoubtedly I should keep watch, for we must be in the very heart of enemy territory. But this time I could not fight the demands of my body. My eyelids closed against my will —I fell asleep.

inner chill which my thermo clothing was no proof against.
My hands moved over fur engrimed with dust and grit. I
looked down. The glassia head rose from its pillow on my
arm.

"Maelen?" So vivid had that dream been that I half
expected to find her still as she had been moments ago.

"Look yonder!"

She used her nose as a pointer to indicate the globes.
Some of those were glowing brighter, giving more light to
the chamber. It took me only a moment or two to be sure
that not all of them had so awakened—just those with the
reptilian design.

"Griss!" I put the only name I knew to that menace.

"Griss Sharvan?" Her thought was surprised. "What has
this to do with him?"

"Much, perhaps." Swiftly I told her of what had happened to me since I had been taken captive by that thing
wearing Griss's body, and of the visit to the crystal-walled
chamber where he had endeavored to give my body to his
fellow being.

"She is also there, is she not?" Maelen asked.

I did not mistake her. There was only one "she"—the
woman of the cat crown.

"Yes! And, Maelen, just now I dreamed—"

"I know what manner of dream that was, since it also
spun me into its web," she interrupted again. "I had
thought that no one could surpass the Thassa in inner
powers. But it would seem that in some things we are as
children playing with bright pebbles, making patterns on
the earth! I think that these have slept here to preserve their
race against some great peril in the past. But only those

four you have seen survived, able to rise to full life again."

"But if they can be revived, why do they want our bodies?"

"It can be that the means of revival on their own cannot now be used. Or it may be that they wish to pass among us as beings of our own kind."

"To take over." That I could believe. Had the seeming Griss Sharvan concealed his alienness, posed perhaps as a captive among the jacks, we would have been deceived and so in saving him could have brought disaster among ourselves. I thought of the men I had left behind on the cliff. They were facing worse than jack blasters—and now I was impatient to be away, to warn them.

I had found Maelen. Now we must find our way out, return to the *Lydis*, or to the force of our men. What was happening here was vastly larger and worse than any jack looting!

"You are right." Maelen had followed my thoughts. "But as to discovering the path out—that I do not know. Can you even now find the door which you entered?"

"Of course!" Though I could not see any opening, I was sure I knew just where I had come through to this ledge. Gently I lifted her aside and arose. To make certain I would not miss what I sought if the opening were disguised in some manner, I put my fingers to the surface of the wall and edged along back toward that place where I thought I had entered.

I reached the far end of the ledge. There was no opening. Sure that I had made some mistake, yet somehow equally certain I could not have, I made a slow passage back, this time reaching both above and below my former tracing of of the surface. I returned to Maelen. There had been no break in that solid wall.

"But I *did* come through!" I burst out, and my protest echoed hollowly through that space.

"True. But where?" Her question seemed a mockery of my vehemence.

Then she continued. "Such an experience is not unknown here. This has happened to me twice. Which is why I have been so completely lost."

"Tell me!" I demanded now.

So I learned how she had made her way from the ship valley, found the sleeper with the amplifier, how she had come to witness the looting of the cache, even as I guessed it might all have happened. But for the rest it was a tale of a strange journey, of her will battling that of another reaching out for her. Not, she felt, for her personally, but as one might fling a net in hope of catching something within it. But that compulsion was not continuous in its powers and she was able to fight it at intervals. It had brought her to where the ship of the jacks was finned down, and through the cavern there into the passages beyond. But there, bemused by the ebb and flow of the current which held her, she had been lost. Then she had contacted me, had been drawn toward my call in turn.

"I had believed that Thassa could not be so influenced," she admitted frankly. "Always I have been warned that I was too proud of my powers. If that was ever so, it is no longer. For here I have been as one played with by something infinitely greater, allowed to run a little, then put under restraint again. Yet this is the strangest of all, Krip— I will swear by the Word of Molaster that this power, this energy, whatever it may be, was not as conscious of me as I am of it. It was rather as if it flexed muscles in exercise so that it might be ready to use all its strength at a future call."

"The four of that inner place?" I suggested.

"Perhaps. Or they may be only extensions of something else, infinitely greater still. They are adepts, without question—very powerful ones. But even an adept recognizes something above and beyond himself. We name Molaster in our petitions. But that is only our name for what we cannot describe, but which is the core of our belief. These others are—"

What she might have added to her speculations was left unsaid. Those yellow globes with the reptilian masks, which had been glowing so much brighter, now gave off a low, humming note. And that sound, subdued as it was, startled us into immobility. We crouched, breathing only shallowly, our heads going right to left, left to right, as we went on guard against what this change might herald.

"Where is the door out?" I demanded.

"Perhaps you can guess better than I have been able to. Even as you, I went from dark to light, found this ledge, but no return. When your mind-send came I hoped it would direct me to an exit. But that was not to be. You came to me instead."

"Where did you come in?"

Her nose pointed to the other end of the ledge, well away from the spot where I was still sure my door existed. I went there, again running palms and fingers along the surface, hunting the smallest hint of an opening. I still had the cutter which Maelen had used on the tangler cords. Perhaps with that, or one of the other tools from my belt, I could force a lock, were I able to find it. A forlorn hope, but one clings to such.

The humming from the globes was continuous now. And it did something to my hearing. Or was there a more subtle outflow rising beyond the range of audibility to affect my thinking? Twice I found I had halted my search, was standing, gazing down at the globes, my mind seemingly blanked out. It could only have lasted a second or two, but it was frightening.

Now I believed that the globes were generating a haze. The forbidding representation of the designs on them was fading. However, that concealment acted in a strange way, just the opposite of what one might expect. One could no longer see those monsters, their elongated jaws a fraction open, their formidable fangs revealed, yet there was the feeling that so hidden, they were more alive!

"Krip!" Maelen's thought-cry dispelled what was building in my mind. I was able to look away, turn my head back to the wall. But now I feared that a danger worse than imagination presented was threatening us.

Solid wall. I thumped it now with my fist as I went, my blows faster, more savage. All they brought me was bruises and pain. Until—I had carried in mind so sharply the thought of a door, the need for a door—my fist went through!

To my eyes the stone was solid, as solid as it had ever been. But my hand had sunk in up to the wrist.

"Maelen!"

She needed no call. She was already padding toward me. Door—where had the invisible door come from?

"Think *door*—think it! See a door in your mind!"

I obeyed her. Door—there was a door there—of course
there was. My hand had gone through the opening. There
might be an illusion to deceive the eye, but there was
nothing now to baffle touch. I rested my other hand on
Maelen's head and we moved resolutely forward together
into what appeared solid, unbroken stone.

Again we passed abruptly from light to dark. But also,
as if a portal had slammed shut behind us, the humming
was instantly silenced. I gave a sigh of relief.

"Is this your way?" I asked. Though how she could be
certain of that in the dark, I did not know.

"I cannot be sure. But it is *a* way. We must keep together."

I left my hand on her head as she crowded against me.
So linked, we went on, very slowly and cautiously, my
other hand outstretched before me to warn of anything
which might rise in our path.

Shortly thereafter I found a wall, traced along it until
there was another way open to the left. Long ago I had lost
all sense of direction, and Maelen confessed to a similar
disability. We could do little until we found some lighted
way. That we might not do so was a horror we refused to
give mind-room to.

Whether the Thassa shared the ancient fear of the dark
with my own race, I did not know. But the sense of com-
pression, of stiffling pressure, returned. Save that this time I
did not walk with my arms bound to my sides.

"Left now—"

"Why? How do you know?"

"Life force in that direction."

I tried mind-probe for myself. She was right—a flicker

of energy. It was not the high flow I associated with the
aliens, but more like such as I could pick up when not too
far from a crew member. And there was an opening to the
left.

How far we were from the chamber of the globes now I
could not guess. But a lighting of the way cheered us—and
that grew ever brighter.

Only now there was sound also. Not a mutter of voices,
but rather the clank of metal. Maelen pushed against me.

"He, the one who wears Griss's body—ahead!"

I tried no probe. I wished I could do just the opposite,
reduce all mental activity so far down the scale he could
not pick up any hint of us in return. I had not forgotten
how easily he had found me out when I had spied on the
jacks.

"He is one-minded now," Maelen told me, "using all his
power for something which is of very great importance to
him. We need not fear him, for he puts all to one purpose."

"And that?"

She did not reply at once. Then—

"Lend me of your sending—"

It was my turn to hesitate. To strengthen any mind-seek
she might send out could make us more accessible to discovery. Yet I trusted her enough to realize that she would
not suggest such a move unless she thought we had a fair
chance. So I yielded.

Her probe sped out, and I fed my own energy to it. This
we had not often done, so it was a relatively new experience
for me, bringing with it an odd sensation of being pulled
along in a current I could not fight. Then a blurred mind-
picture came.

We seemed to be hanging in the air over a pit, or rather we were in the apex of one of those pyramid chambers. Below a robo was blasting away at the foot of one wall. There was already a dark cavity there; now the machine was enlarging that.

Behind the worker stood Griss. He did not hold any control board. It would appear that he was able to keep the robo at work without that. And his attention was com-pletely absorbed by what he was doing. But that feverish desire which drove him was like a broadcast. He did not hold his defenses now, but fastened avidly on what he sought —an ancient storehouse of his kind, perhaps containing machines or weapons. His need was like a whiff of ozone. A whiff, I say, because I caught only the edge of it. Around the chamber, well above the level at which the robo worked, was another of the ledge ways. This ran across one wall, leading from one door to another. And without needing to to be told, I recognized that this was the path we must follow.

Whether we could do it without attracting attention from below was another matter. But now that hole the robo battered was larger. The machine wheeled back, became inert. And the alien hurried to the break, disappeared through it.

"Now!"

We sped along the lighted corridor, and it was only a short distance until we ventured out on that ledge. It was so close to the apex of the pyramid that the opposite wall leaned very close. Maelen found it easier to take that route than I, for I could not stand erect but had to go on hands and knees.

Nor did I waste any time looking back at the hole the robo had opened. To reach the door on the other side, scramble within, was all I wanted.

"We made it!"

"For now, yes," she answered me. "But—"

She swung around, her head down. Her dusty body quivered.

"Krip! Krip, hold me!" It was a cry for help, coming so suddenly, without warning, that I was startled. Then I half threw myself over her, grasping her tightly around the body, holding on in spite of her struggles for freedom.

It was no longer Maelen whom I held so, but an animal that growled and snapped, struck out with unsheathed claws. Only by pure chance did I escape harm. Then she collapsed against me, her breath coming in deep gasps. There were flecks of white foam at the corners of her jaws.

"Maelen, what is it?"

"The calling—it was stronger this time, much stronger. Like—like to like!"

"What do you mean?" I still held her but she was far from fighting now. As if her struggle had exhausted her, she was in nearly the same condition in which I had earlier found her.

"The dream—she of the cat crown." Maelen's thoughts did not make a completely coherent pattern. "She is—akin to Thassa—"

But I refused to believe that. I could see no resemblance between her and the Maelen I had known.

"Maybe not to the sight," Maelen agreed. "Krip—is there more water?" She was still panting, the sound of it close to human sobbing. I found the flask, poured a little

in her mouth. But some I must save, for we did not know
when we could replenish that small supply.

She swallowed greedily, but she did not press me for
more.

"The mind-call—the dream—I knew their like. Such are
of Thassa kind."

I had a flash of inspiration. "Could it be adjusted? That
is—having discovered you, could the pattern be altered to
a familiar one, thus with a better chance of entrapping
you?"

"That may well be so," she admitted. "But between me
and that other there is something— Only when I face
her, it will be on my terms and not hers, if you will give
me of your strength as you did this time when she called."

"You are sure it was she? Not the one we just saw?"

"Yes. But when I go it will be at a time of *my* choosing.
Which is not yet."

Having taken a mouthful of water myself, I brought out
an E-ration tube, which we shared half and half. Made for
nourishment during times of strain, it was high in suste-
nance and would keep us going for hours to come.

There was no sound from the chamber where the robo
must still be on guard beside that hole. I wondered very
much what the alien sought beyond the battered wall. But
Maelen did not mention that as we went. On the contrary,
she asked a question so much apart from the matters at
hand I was startled.

"Do you think her fair?"

Her? Oh, I realized, she must mean the alien woman.

"She is very beautiful," I answered frankly.

"A body without blemish—though strange in its coloring. A perfect body—"

"But its mind reaches for another covering. That which walks in Griss was also perfect outwardly, yet its rightful owner saw fit to exchange with Griss. And I was taken there to exchange with another one. Are they in stass-freeze, I wonder?"

"Yes." She was definite. "That other one, he whom they used on the cliff top—"

"Lukas said he was dead—long dead. But those four, I am sure they are alive. The one in Griss *must* be!"

"Perhaps it may be that their bodies, once released from stass-freeze, will truly die. But I do not think so. I believe that they wish to preserve those for some other reason. And they seek our bodies as we would put on meaner clothes which may be soiled and thrown away once some dirty job is finished. But—she is very beautiful!"

There was a wistfulness in that, one of those infrequent displays of what appeared to be human emotion on Maelen's part. And such always moved me the more because they came so seldom. So I believed her a little subject to the same desires as my own species.

"Goddess, queen—what was she, or who?" I wondered. "We cannot guess her real name."

"Yes, her name." Maelen repeated my thought in part. "That she would not want us to know."

"Why? Because"—and I thought then of the old superstition—"that would give us power over her? But that is the belief of a primitive people! And I would say she is far from primitive."

"I have told you, Krip"—Maelen was impatient—"belief is important. Belief can move the immovable if it is rightly applied. Should a people believe that one's name is so personal a possession that to know it gives another power over one, then for them that is true. And from world to world degrees of civilization differ as much as customs and names for gods."

My head was up now, and I sniffed, alerted once again by a scent rather than a sound. Maelen must have been quick to catch the same trace of odor.

"Ahead—others. Perhaps their camp."

Where there was a camp there must also be some communication with the outer world. And I wanted nothing so much as to be free of these burrows, to return to the *Lydis*. At least my sojourn here had given me knowledge enough to warn and arouse my fellows to such danger as we had not known existed. So—if we did want to escape the heart of the enemy's territory, we must still push on into what might be open danger.

But I had not realized that my own wanderings must have been in a circle. For when we came to a doorway we were looking out into the cavern of the jack camp. The looted chests were piled about, and we could see, in the outer air before the entrance, a portion of the ship's fins.

There was a line of robos, all idle now, to the right. No sign of any men about. If we could keep to cover behind the boxes we might reach the outer opening—

But one step, or at the most two, at a time. Maelen was slinking, with her belly fur brushing the floor, along behind that line of empty chests. And I crouched as low as I could to join her. There was no sound; we could be totally alone.

But we dared not depend on such good fortune. And it was well that we did not, for the side of the plasta-bubble tent parted as its entrance was unsealed and a man came out.

When I saw him I froze. Harkon—and not a prisoner. He carried a blaster openly, had turned to look back over his shoulder, as if waiting for someone else. Had the party from the *Lydis* taken, by some miracle of fortune, the headquarters of the jacks? If so, they must be speedily warned of what wore Griss's body. I had no illusions as to what would happen if that confronted them. The odds might be ten to one against that alien and yet he would come out the winner.

Chapter 12

MAELEN

We are told that all the universe lies on the balance of Molaster's unseen scales—good weighs against bad, ill against well. And when it seems to us most likely that fortune has turned, that is the time to be most wary. I had met much which was new to me since I had put on Vors's body and come to be one of this band of off-worlders. Yet I had always supposed that the core of the balance remained the same and that only the outer forms differed.

However, in these underground ways I had avoided challenges and learned things which were so outside the reference of all I had known before that many times I could only make blind choices. And to a Moon Singer of the Thassa a blind choice is an affront and a defeat.

Twice I had dreamed true—I could not be deceived in that—of her whom Krip had actually looked upon. Why was she so familiar to me when I had never seen her like before? There were no women on the *Lydis*, and those I had met on the three planets we had visited since first I raised from Yiktor were no different from the females of the plains people—never more than pale copies of what their men desired, creatures without rights or many thoughts.

But she—there was in me such a longing, a drive, to go and look upon her in body even as I had in dream, that I ever struggled against that compulsion, nor did I reveal it wholly to Krip. But that he had shared my second dream was to me proof that danger lay in actually facing her and I must not risk a confrontation yet. For what he had to tell me of the fate they had intended for him was a warning. I believe that it was perhaps that small bit of Thassa lurking in him which had defeated the takeover they had planned.

During the months we had voyaged together I had realized that Krip was a greater esper than he had been at our first meeting. It was my thought that this slow awakening of power, this development of his talent, was influenced by Maquad's body. Though I did not know how or why. Which again gave me to think about what a long indwelling in my present form might do to *me!*

I knew that the aliens had not been able to dispossess him, that the encased creature had ordered him taken away as a possible danger. And that small fact was the only favorable thing I had to hold to—save that we were together again and had found the door to the outer world.

It was pleasing that Krip did not move at once into the open when we saw the Patrolman. His care to remain in hiding, willing to accept nothing and no one unproved, reassured me. So we lay behind the boxes watching. Nor did either of us use mind-send. For if this Patrolman was not

what he seemed, we would be thus betrayed to greater
peril than we had lately been in.

Harkon moved away from the bubble and another came
out—Juhel Lidj of the *Lydis*. He, too, carried his weapon;
still, about both of them there was no sign that they feared
any enemy. They were too much at their ease. And yet
they were both men who had faced danger many times over,
not foolhardy adventurers.

Together they passed us, moving toward the back of the
cave and the mouth of one of the dark ways there. Still
Krip did not stir nor try to hail them, and I waited his lead.
But he edged around to watch them go. When he could be
sure they were out of sight his hand touched my head for a
close communication which could not be heard.

"They—I have a feeling all is wrong—not right."

"So do I," I was quick to answer.

"Could they have been taken over also? It is best we try
to reach the *Lydis*. But if I have guessed wrong, and they
are walking straight into what lies there—" I felt him
shiver, his fingers on my head tremble slightly.

"If they are as you fear now, then they are masters here,
and should they discover us— But if the others are still
free from such contamination they must be warned. For the
present we can hope such domination is confined to Sekhmet. Have you thought what might happen if their ship
out there lifts off, carrying those who can change bodies as
easily as you change the clothing on your back—spreading
the contagion of their presence to other worlds?"

"Such evil as has never been known before. And there
could be no finding them once they were off this planet!"

"Therefore—carry your message while still you may." In

this I was urging what I had decided was the greater good. There was nothing one man and one glassia could do in these burrows to overset such enemies, but there was much which we could accomplish elsewhere.

"They could already have started it," he said then. "How do we know how many there are of them—how many voyages that ship out there has made?"

"The more reason why a warning must be given."

We were on the move again, using the looted chests as a shield as long as we could. Then we came into the pallid daylight at the cavern's entrance.

The cargo hatches of the ship were sealed, but her passenger ramp was still out. Krip looked up at her. He was far more knowledgeable of such than I. To me she merely seemed larger than the *Lydis*, and so I said.

"She is. We are D class; this is a C class ship, also a freighter, a converted Company freighter. She is slow, but can lift far more than the *Lydis*. And she has no insignia, which means she is a jack ship."

There were no guards to be seen, but we still kept to cover. And the broken nature of the country seemed designed to aid such skulking. That and the fact that the clouds were very dense overhead and a cold, ice-toothed rain began to fall. Shivering under the lash of that, we found a place where we could climb the cliff. We thought prudence dictated such an exit rather than use of the rough road beaten by many robo tracks.

Aloft, I could trust for our guide to the sense which was a part of Vors's natural equipment, and we headed in the direction where I was sure we would find the *Lydis*. But it was a nightmare of a journey, with the sleet sluicing around

us and the dark growing thicker. We crawled where we
longed to run, afraid of missteps which would plunge us
over some rock edge.

There was a wind rising. I unsheathed claws to anchor me
and crept close to the ground under the beating of its force
and that of the sleet.

"Krip?" Here four clawed feet might manage, but I was
not sure that two booted ones might do as well. And the
fury of this storm was like nothing I had felt before. It was
almost as if the natural forces of this forsaken world were
ranged on the side of those who looted.

"Keep on!" There was no weakness in his reply.

I had come to a down slope where the water poured in
streams about me as I twisted and turned, using every possible hint of protection against the worst blasts. As I went
I began to doubt very gravely if we could press on to the
Lydis, wonder whether it would not be much more prudent
to seek shelter and wait out the worst of this storm. And I
was about to look for a place where we could do so, when
the stones my claws rasped were no longer firm, but slid,
carrying me with them.

Over—out—into nothingness! An instant of knowing
that I was falling—then a blast of pain and darkness.

Yet that dark was not complete, and I carried with me an
instant of raw, terrifying knowledge—that it had been no
normal misstep, no chance which had brought me down. I
had been caught in a trap I had not suspected.

And, recognizing that, I knew also why it had been done
and the full danger of what might follow.

But with Sharvan, again with Krip on Yiktor, there had

been an exchange of bodies. Why need my present one be destroyed—why?

How better to enforce slavery upon an identity than by destroying the body which it inhabited?

Pain! Such pain as I had not believed could exist in a sane world. And in no way would my body obey me.

"Cannot—can never now—"

The message reaching me was erratic, such as a faulty line of communication would make.

"Leave—come—come—come!"

"Where? For what purpose?"

"Life force—life force! Live again—come!"

I made the great effort of my life, trying to cut off the pain of my body, to center all my energy and will on that which was the core of my identity.

"Come—your body dies—come!"

Thereby that which called made its grave error. All living things have a fear of being blotted out, of nonexistence. It is part of our armor, to keep us ever alert against evil, knowing that we have a certain way to walk and that how we walk it judges us on Molaster's scales. We do not give up easily. But also the White Road has no terrors for the Thassa, if the time has come for us to step onto its way. This which had entrapped me played upon the fear of nonexistence, as if those with whom it had had earlier dealings could visualize no other life beyond what men call death. Thus it would readily gain what it wanted by offering life continuation quickly at the moment when that death approached.

"Come!" Urgency in that. "Would you be nothing?"

So I read its great need. My identity was not what it wished to take to itself, nor did it seek another's body. For to it its own covering was a treasure it clung to. No, it wanted my life force as a kind of fuel that, drawing upon this force, it might live again on its own terms.

"Maelen! Maelen, where are you?"

"Come!"

"Maelen!"

Two voices in my head, and the pain rising again! Molaster! I gave my own cry for help, trying not to hear either of those other calls. And there came an answer—not the White Road, no. That I could have if I willed it. But such a choice would endanger another plan. That was made clear to me as if I had been lifted once more to the cliff crest and a vast scene of action spread before me. What I saw then I could not remember, even as I looked upon it. But that it was needful, I knew. And also I understood that I must struggle to fulfill my part in that purpose.

"Come!" No coaxing, no promises now—just an order delivered as if it could not possibly be disobeyed. "Come now!"

But I answered that other call of my name, sent my own plea.

"Here—hurry!" How I might carry out the needful task I did not know. Much would depend now upon the skill and resources of another.

I could not make the glassia body obey me or even give me sight. To keep my mind clear, I had to block off all five senses lest pain drive me completely forth. But my mind—that much I had—for a space.

"Krip!" Whether he was still on the cliff top or beside

me, I had no means of knowing. Only I must reach him and give him this last message or all would fail. "Krip— this body—I think it is too badly broken—it is dying. But it must not die yet. If you can get it into stass-freeze— You must! That box with the sleeper—get me to that—"

I could not even wait for any answer to my message. I must just hold grimly, as long as I could. And how long that might be—only Molaster could set limit to.

It was a strange hidden place where that which was the real "I"—Maelen of the Thassa, Moon Singer once, glassia once—held and drew upon all inner resources. Did that other still batter at my defenses, crying "Come, come— live"? I did not know. I dared not think of anything save holding fast to this small stronghold which was under attack. Weaker grew my hold so that at times the pain struck in great punishing blows. Then I tried only to form the words of singing, which I had not done since they took away my wand. And the words were like dim, glowing coals where once they had been leaping flames of light. Yet still there was a feeble life in them and they sustained me, damping out the pain.

There was no time in this place—or else far too much of it. I assured myself, "I can hold one more instant, and one more, and one more"—and so it continued. Whether Krip could accomplish that which would save me, or *if* it would save me— But I must think of nothing save the need to hold on, to keep my identity in this hidden place. I must hold and hold and hold!

But I could no longer— Molaster! Great were the powers once given me, much did I increase them by training. But there comes an end to all—and that faces me now. I have lost, I cannot remember that pattern of life which I was shown. Though I know its importance and know that not by the will of the Great Design was it interrupted for me. Yet it would seem that I have not the strength to finish out my part of it. I—cannot—hold—

Pain rushed in as a great scarlet wave to drown me.

"Maelen!"

One voice only now. Had that other given up? But I thought that even yet, were I to yield, it would sweep me into its web.

"Maelen!"

"Freeze—" I could shape only that one last plea. And so futile, so hopeless a one it was. There came no answer.

None—save that the pain grew less, now almost bearable. And I had not been cut free from the body. What—

"Maelen!"

I was in the body still. Though I did not command it, yet it served as an anchor. And there was a freedom from that pressure which had been upon me. As if the process of my "death" had been arrested, and I was to be given a short breathing space.

"Maelen!" Imperative, imploring—that call.

I summoned up the dregs of my energy.

"Krip—freeze—"

"Yes, Maelen. You are in the case—the case of the alien. Maelen—what—"

So—he had done it. He had taken that last small chance and it was the right one. But I had no time for rejoicing, not now. I must let him know the final answer.

"Keep freeze—Old Ones—Yiktor—"

My hold on consciousness, if one could term that state of rigid defense "consciousness," broke. Did I walk the White Road now? Or was there still a place for me in the great pattern?

Chapter 13

KRIP VORLUND

The wind could not reach fully here, still my hands were numb. I watched the box. How I had ever mastered its catches, opened it long enough to pull out the body it had contained and put the broken, limp, bloodied bundle of fur in its place, I did not know. I shook with shock more than with chill, weak with the effort of transporting what had been Maelen across the rocky way, sure that she—that no living thing could survive such handling in the state I found her after that terrible fall. Yet she had lived, she was in freeze now. And I swore she would get to Yiktor— to the Old Ones—that she was not going to die! Though how I might do this I did not know.

I edged around. There stood the *Lydis* far below, the two flitters. No sign of life about them. Something else lay here among the rocks. I stared, and my shudders grew worse. The alien I had pulled so hastily from the freeze box—

But no body lay there—only a crumbling mass. I covered

my eyes. Lukas had said it was dead, and his words were being proved now. Not that it mattered—nothing did, save Maelen. And the warning which must be delivered. Harkon, Lidj—were they still men or— And who else? All those who had gone out against an enemy infinitely stronger than we had suspected?

I put out my hand to the freeze box as gently as I might have laid it on a furred head.

"I cannot take you with me now," I thought. Perhaps I could still reach her, perhaps not. But I had to try to make her understand that I was not deserting her. "I shall be back—and you shall see Yiktor, the Old Ones—live again. I swear it!"

Then I set about wedging that box even more tightly among the rocks, making very sure that it could not be shifted by any freak of wind or storm. If she was safe now, that covering must endure until I could fulfill my promise.

Having done what I could to ensure her protection, I descended through the lashing of wind and sleet to the floor of the valley. Reaching there, I used my wrist com, clicking out the code which ought to open the *Lydis* to me, waiting tensely for some sign that the call had been heard within the ship.

My answer came, not from the ship, but out of the night. A flash beam cut the black, pinned me against the rock wall of the cliff. Jacks—they had beaten me here!

I was so dazzled by that ray that I could not see who was behind it, though I believed they were moving in for the kill. I had no weapon now. Then someone stepped out into the light beam and I saw the uniform. Patrol! Only now that could be no reassurance either. Not since I had seen

Harkon and Lidj in the cavern and knew what walked in Griss's body.

I tried to read in his face whether he was what he seemed or one of the enemy, but there was no clue in either eyes or expression. He motioned with his hand. The howling of the wind was far too loud to allow speech, but his gesture was toward the *Lydis*. Then the beam flashed downward, pointing a path to the ship, the upper edge of it catching the slow descent of the ramp. I went.

The *Lydis* had been my home for years, and I had felt privileged that that was so. But now, as I climbed her ramp, using handholds to drag myself up against the sweep of the wind, it was as if I approached something alien, with a whiff of trap about it. It could be just that, if the contagion of the aliens had spread this far.

I found myself sniffing as I came through the lock, the Patrolman behind me, as if I could actually scent that alien evil I feared to find here. But there was only the usual smell of a star ship. I began to climb the ladder to the control cabin. What would I find there?

"Vorlund!"

Captain Foss. And beyond him a Patrol officer with the stellar sword badge of a commander. Others— Though it was on Foss I centered my attention. If it *was* Foss. How could I be sure? What might have happened during that endless time I wandered underground? I did not answer but only stared at him, searching his face for any hint that he was not the man I knew.

Then one of the Patrolmen who had followed me up the ladder took me by the arm, turned me a little as if I were totally helpless, and pushed me down into the astrogator's chair, which swung as my weight settled in it. I dared to try mind-probe—for I had to know if there was yet time.

"You *are* Foss!" My voice sounded thin, hardly above a whisper.

Then I saw his expression change, recognized that slight lift of one brow—something I had seen many times in the past.

"You were expecting someone else?" he asked.

"One of them." I was near to babbling, suddenly so tired, so drained of energy. "Like Griss—one of them—inside your body."

No one spoke. Had I said that at all, or only thought it?

Then the captain turned to the emergency dispenser on the wall, twirled its dial, brought out a sustain tube. He came over to me. I tried to raise my hand to take that restorative. My body would not obey. He held it to my mouth and I drank. The stuff was hot, fighting the chill and shaking weariness in me.

"One of them—inside my body?" he said as if that were the most natural condition. "Perhaps you had better explain."

"Back there." I gestured to the wall of the *Lydis*, hoping I was indicating the direction of the burrows. "Aliens. They can take over our bodies. They did with Griss. He's —he's in the alien body now—behind a wall. He—" I shut out that memory of Griss imprisoned in the motionless body wearing the reptilian crown. "I think maybe Lidj, Harkon, too. They were too much at ease there in the cavern, as if they had nothing to fear. Maybe others— They tried to do it with me—didn't work. The alien was angry, said I was dangerous—to put me in the dark— Then I found Maelen."

Maelen! In that freeze box—on the cliff. Maelen!

"What about Maelen?" Foss had taken the pilot's seat so that his eyes were now on a level with mine. He sat forward, and his hands took mine from where they lay limp, holding them in a firm, warm grip. "What happened to Maelen?"

I sensed a stir, as if the Patrol officer moved closer. Foss frowned, not at me.

"What about Maelen, Krip?"

"She fell—onto the rocks—all broken. Dying—she was dying! Told me—must freeze—freeze until I could get her home, back to Yiktor. I took her—all broke, broken—" I tried to sever the compelling stare with which he held me, to forget that nightmare of a journey, but he would not let me. "Took her to the alien—opened the box—took the alien's body out—put her in. She was still alive—then."

"These aliens." Foss's voice was level, clear. He held me by it as well as by the grip on my hands and wrists. "Do you know who they are?"

"Lukas said dead—a long time. But they are esper. And the crowned ones are not dead. Bodies—they want bodies! Griss, for sure, maybe the others. There are four of them —I saw—counting the woman."

"He doesn't make sense!" cut in an impatient voice.

Again Foss frowned in warning. "Where are these bodies?"

"Underground—passages—rooms. The jacks have a camp —in a cavern—ship outside. They were looting—rooms with chests." Memories made dizzy, whirling pictures in my head. I had a bitter taste in my mouth as if the restorative was rising now to choke me.

"Where?"

"Beyond the cache. I got in through the cat's mouth." I tried to control that nausea, to remain coherent. "Passage there. But they—Griss—can hold men with thought alone. If the rest are like him, you have no chance. Never met an esper like him before, not even Thassa. Maelen thought they could not take me over because I am part Thassa now. But they did take me prisoner—Griss did—just by willing it. They used a tangler on me after."

"Korde." Foss gave a swift order. "Scrambler on—highest frequency!"

"Yes, sir!"

Scrambler, I thought vaguely—scrambler? Oh, yes, defense against probes. But would it work against the thing in Griss's body?

"About the others." The Patrol commander had moved around behind Foss. "Where are the others—my men—yours?"

"I don't know. Only saw Griss, Harkon, Lidj—"

"And you think that Harkon and Lidj may also be taken over?"

"Saw them walking around in jack camp, not taking any precautions. Had the feeling they had no reason to fear discovery."

"Did you probe them?"

"Didn't dare. Probe, and if they were taken over, they would have taken us, Maelen and me. Griss—he knew I was there even before he saw me. He made me walk out into their hands. But—they acted as if they belonged in that camp. And there was no sign of the others with them."

I saw Foss nod. "Perhaps the right guess. You can sense danger."

"Take you over," I repeated. The restorative was no longer working. I was slipping away, unable to keep my eyes open. "Maelen—" They must help Maelen!

Chapter 14

KRIP VORLUND

There was no night or day in the interior of the *Lydis*, but I had that dazed feeling that one has when one has slept very heavily. I put up one hand to deliver the usual greeting rap on the side of the upper bunk. If Maelen had slept too—

Maelen! Her name unlocked memory and I sat up without caution, knocking my head painfully against the low-slung upper bunk. Maelen was still out there—in the freeze box! She must be brought in, put under such safeguards as the ship could give. How had I come to forget about her?

I was already on my feet, reaching for the begrimed thermo clothing dropped in a heap on the floor, when the door panel opened. I looked around to see the captain.

Foss was never one to reveal his thoughts on his face. A top Trader learns early to dissemble or to wear a mask. But there are small signs, familiar to those who live in close company, which betray strong emotions. What I

saw now in Foss was a controlled anger which I had known
only once or twice during the time I had shipped on board
the *Lydis*.

Deliberately he entered my cabin without invitation.
That act in itself showed the gravity of the situation. For
privacy is so curtailed on board a spacer that each member
of the crew is overly punctilious about any invasion of another's. He pulled down one of the wall seats and sat in
it, still saying nothing.

But I was in no mood to sit and talk, if that was his
intention. I wanted Maelen as safe as I could make her.
I had no idea how long I had slept, leaving her exposed
to danger.

Since the captain seemed in no hurry to announce his
business with me, I broke silence first.

"I must get Maelen. She is in an alien freeze box—up
on the cliffs. I must get her into our freeze compartment
—" As I spoke I sealed my thermo jacket. But Foss made
no move to let me by, unless I physically pushed him aside.

"Maelen—" Foss repeated her name, but there was
something so odd about the tone of his voice that he caught
my attention in spite of my impatience to be gone.

"Vorlund, how did it come about that you weren't with
the rest—that you found your own way into that chain of
burrows? You left here in company." His eyes held mine in
intent measuring. Perhaps, had my mind not been largely
on the need for reaching Maelen, I might have been uneasy,
or taken partial warning from both his question and his
attitude.

"I left them on the cliff top. Maelen called—she was in
trouble."

"I see." He was still watching me with a measuring look, as if I were a piece of merchandise he had begun to suspect was not up to standard. "Vorlund—" Suddenly he reached up and pressed a stud. The small locking cupboard sprang open. As the inner side of the door was a mirror, I found myself staring at my own face.

It always gave me a feeling almost of shock to see my reflection thus. After so many years of facing one image, it takes time to get used to another. My skin was somewhat browner than it had been on Yiktor. Yet it in no way matched the dark space tan which all the other crew members had and which I had once accepted as proper. Against even the slightest coloring my silver brows, slanting up to join the hairline on my temples, and the very white locks there, close-cropped as they were, had no resemblance to my former appearance. I now had the delicately boned Thassa face, the pointed chin.

"Thassa." Foss's word underlined what I saw reflected. "You told us on Yiktor that bodies did not matter, that you were still Krip Vorlund."

"Yes," I said when he paused, as if his words had a deep meaning to be seriously considered. "I am Krip Vorlund. Did I not prove it?"

Could he possibly think now that I was really Thassa? That I had managed to masquerade successfully all these months among men who knew me intimately?

"Are you? The Krip Vorlund, Free Trader, that we knew would not put an alien above his ship—or his duty!"

I was shaken. Not only because he would say and think such a thing of me, but because there was truth in it! Krip Vorlund would not have left that squad on the cliff top

—gone to answer Maelen. Or would he? But I *was* Krip. Or was it true, that shadowy fear of mine, that something of Maquad governed me?

"You see," Foss continued, "you begin to understand. You are not, as you swore to us, Krip Vorlund. You are something else. And this being so—"

I turned from the mirror to face him squarely. "You think I let the men down in some way? But I tell you, *I* would not have dared use esper—not around what controls Griss Sharvan now. Only such as Maelen might dare that. And *his* change was certainly none of my doing. If I had not acted as I did, would you have your warning now?"

"Only you did not go off on your own for us, to do our scouting."

I was silent, because again he was speaking the truth. Then he continued:

"If enough of Krip is left in you to remember our ways, you know that what you did was not Trader custom. What you appear to be is a part of you now."

That thought was as chilling as the fear I had faced in the burrows. If Foss saw me as an alien, what did I have left? Yet I could not allow that to influence me. So I turned on him with the best argument I could muster.

"Maelen is part of our safeguard. Such esper powers as hers are seldom at the service of any ship. Remember, it was she who smashed that amplifier up on the cliff, the one which held us all prisoner while you were gone. If we have to face these aliens it may be Maelen who will decide the outcome for us. She is crew! And she was in danger and called. Because I can communicate with her best, I heard her and I went."

"Logical argument." Foss nodded. "What I would expect, Vorlund. But you and I both know that there is more standing behind such words than you have mentioned."

"We can argue that out later, once we are free from Sekhmet." Trader code or not, I was ridden by the need to get Maelen into what small safety the *Lydis* promised. "But Maelen has to be brought to our freeze unit—now!"

"I'll grant you that." To my vast relief the captain arose. Whether he accepted my plea that Maelen was crew, that her gifts were for our benefit, I could not tell. It was enough for the present that he would go to her aid.

I do not know what arguments he used with the Patrol to get them to help us, because I left him behind as I climbed to the cliff crest. There was no alien face behind the frostless top plate now. Maelen's small body took so little room in the box it was out of sight. My quick inspection of the fastenings proved that the container had not been disturbed since I had left it. And where I had put the alien body, there was nothing at all. The winds must have scoured away the last ashy remains hours ago.

Getting the box down the cliff face was an awkward job, one which we had to do slowly. But at length we brought it up the ramp of the *Lydis* by hand, not entrusting it to the robos. And the Patrol ship's medic waited to make the transfer to the ship's freeze unit.

Every stellar voyaging ship has such a unit to take care of any badly injured until they can be treated at some healing center. But I had not realized, even when I labored to take care of Maelen, how badly broken her glassia body was. And I think that the medic gave up when he saw that bloody bundle of matted fur. But he got a live reading, and that was enough to make him hurry to complete the transfer.

As the hasps locked on the freeze unit, I ran my hand along the top. There was the spark of life still in her; so far had her will triumphed over her body. I did not know how long she might continue to exist so, and the future looked very dark. Could I now possibly get her back to Yiktor? And even if I tracked down the Old Ones of the wandering Thassa and demanded a new body for her, would they give it to me? Where would such a body come from? Another animal form, to fulfill the fate they had set on her? Or perhaps one which was the result of some such case as gave me Maquad's—a body from the care of Umphra's priests, where those injured mentally beyond recovery were tended until Molaster saw fit to set their feet upon the White Road leading them out of the weary torment of their lives?

One step at a time. I must not allow myself to see all the shadows lying ahead. I had Maelen in the best safekeeping possible. In the freeze unit that spark of life within her would be tended with all the care my people knew. A little of the burden had been lifted from me, but much still remained. Now I knew that I owed another debt—as Foss had reminded me. I was ready to pay it as best I could. And I went to the control cabin to offer to do so.

I found Foss, the Patrol commander Borton, and the medic Thanel gathered around a box from which the medic was lifting a loop of wire. From the loop a very delicate collection of metal threads arched back and forth, weaving a cap. He handled this with care, turning it around so that

the light glinted on the threads. Captain Foss looked
around as I came up the ladder.

"We can prove it now. Vorlund is our top esper."

"Good enough. I am a fourth power myself." Thanel
fitted the cap to his own head, the loop resting on his
temples, the fine threads disappearing in his fair hair.

"Mind-send," he ordered me, "highest power."

I tried. But this was like beating against a wall. It was not
the painful, shocking task it had been when I had brushed
against the broadcast of the alien or faced the crowned one;
rather it was like testing a complete shield. I said as much.

Borton had been holding a small object in his hand. Now
he eyed me narrowly. But when he spoke he addressed Foss.

"Did you know he is a seven?"

"We knew he was high, but three trips ago he tested only
a little more than five."

Five to seven! I had not known that. Was that change
because of my Thassa body? Or had constant exchange
with Maelen sharpened and raised my powers?

"You try this." Thanel held out the wire cap and I adjusted it on my head.

All three watched me closely and I could guess that
Thanel was trying mind-send. But I picked up nothing.
It was an odd sensation, as though I had plugged my ears
and was deaf to all around me.

"So it works with a seventh power. But another broadcasting body with an amplifier, and this alien able to
exchange identities, may be even stronger." Borton looked
thoughtful.

"Our best chance." Thanel did not reach for the cap I

still wore. Instead he took out four more. "These are experimental as yet. They held up under lab testing; that's why they have been issued for trial in the field. Sheer luck that we have them at all."

"As far as I can see," Borton observed, "we have little choice. The only alternative is to call in strong arms and blast that installation off Sekhmet. And if we do that we may be losing something worth more than the treasure the jacks have been looting—knowledge. We can't wait for reinforcements, either. Any move to penetrate their stronghold has to come fast, before these body snatchers can rise off-world to play their tricks elsewhere."

"We can get in through the cat's mouth. They may not yet know about that." I offered what I had to give. "I know that way."

In the end it was decided that the cat's mouth did give us the best chance of entering the enemies' territory. And we prepared to risk it. Five men only, as there were only five of the protect caps. Captain Foss represented the sadly dwindled force of the Traders, I was the guide, and the medic Thanel, Commander Borton, and a third from the Patrol force, an expert on X-Tee contacts, comprised our company.

The Patrol produced weapons more sophisticated than any I had ever seen before—an all-purpose laser type which could serve either as a weapon or as a tool. And these were subjected to a very fine adjustment by the electronics officer of the Patrol Scout, so that each would answer only to the finger pressure of the man authorized to carry it. Were it to fall into strange hands it would blow itself apart at the first firing.

Wearing the caps, so armed, and with fresh supplies, we climbed back over the cliffs. Though I could not be aware of any sentries while encapped, we moved with caution, once more a patrol in enemy country. And we spent a long number of moments watching for any sign that the wedge opening of the cat's mouth had been discovered. But the Patrol's persona reader raised no hint that any ambush awaited us there.

I led the way to the opening, once more squirming on my belly into that narrow passage. And as I wriggled forward I listened and watched for any alarm.

Though the first time I had made this journey I had had no way of measuring its length, I began now to wonder about that. Surely we must soon come to the barrier I had opened to allow me into the chamber above the place of the bodies. However, as I crawled on and on, I did not see it— though I carried a torch this time. Doubts of my own memory grew in my mind. Had I not been wearing that cap I would have suspected that I was now under some insidious mental influence.

On and on—yet I did not come to the door, the room beyond. The walls appeared to narrow, though I did not have to push against them any more than I had the first time. Yet the feeling of being caught in a trap increased with every body length that I advanced.

Then the torchlight picked out, not the door I had found before, but a series of notches in the walls, as the surface on which I crept slanted upward. This *was* new, but I had seen no turning in the passage. And there had been no breaks in the original tunnel wall. I was completely lost, but there was nothing to do but keep on. We could not retreat

without great difficulty, strung out as we were without
room to turn.

Those handholds in the wall allowed me to pull myself
along as the incline became much steeper. I still could not
understand what had happened. Only one possible explanation presented itself—that I had been under mental compulsion the *first* time I invaded this space. But the reason
for such confusion? Unless the aliens had devised such a
defense to discourage looters. There were warping devices.
Such were known; they had been found on Atlas—small
there, to be sure, but still working—a device to conceal a
passage from the eye or other senses. There had been
tombs on other worlds which had been protected by all
manner of ingenious devices to kill, maim, or seal up forever those who dared to explore them without knowledge
of their secret safeguards.

And if this was so—what did lie before us now? I could
be leading our small party directly into danger. Yet I was
not sure enough of my deductions to say so. There was a
jerk on one of my boots, nearly strong enough to drag me
backward.

"Where," came a sharp whisper out of the dark, "is this
hall of the sleeping aliens you spoke of?"

A good question, and one for which I had no answer. I
might only evade until I knew more.

"Distances are confusing—it must still lie ahead." I tried
to remember if I had described my other journey in detail.
If so, they must already know this was different. Now I
attempted to speed up my wormlike progress.

The torch showed me an abrupt left turn in the passage
and I negotiated that with difficulty, only to face just such a

barrier as I had found before. With a sigh of relief, I set
my fingers in that hole, tugged the small door open. However, as I crawled through, my hopes were dashed. This was
not the chamber overlooking the hall of the freeze boxes.
Rather I came out in a much wider corridor where a man
might walk upright, but without any other doors along it.
I swung out and tried once again to relate my present surroundings to what I had seen before.

Certainly if I had been under the spell of some hallucin-
atory trick the first time, I would not have been led straight
to one of their places for freezing their army. That should
have been the last place to which they would have wanted
to guide any intruder. Perhaps the Patrol caps, instead of
protecting, had failed completely—so that *this* was the
hallucination?

I had moved away from the entrance. Now, one by one,
the others came through to join me. It was Captain Foss
and Borton who turned upon me.

"Where are we, Vorlund?" Foss asked.

There was nothing left but the truth. "I don't know—"

"This hall of boxed aliens, where is it?"

"I don't know." I had my hand to that tight cap. If I
took it off—what would I see? Was touch as much affected
as sight? Some hallucinations could be so strong that they
enmeshed all the senses. But almost desperately now, I
turned to the rock wall, running my finger tips along its
surface, hoping touch would tell me that this was only an
illusion which I could thereby break.

I was allowed very little time for that inspection. The
tight and punishing grip of Foss's hand brought me around
to face the four I had led here.

"What are you doing?"

Could I ever make them believe that I was as much a victim now as they? That I honestly had no idea of what had happened or why?

"This is not the way I came before. It may be an illusion—

I heard a harsh exclamation from Thanel. "Impossible! The cap would prevent that!"

Borton cut in on the medic. "There is a very simple explanation, captain. It would seem that we have been tricked by your man here." He did not look at me at all now, but rather at Foss, as if he held the captain to account for my actions.

But it was Foss's hand which went swiftly to my belt, disarmed me. And I knew in that moment that all the years of our past comradeship no longer stood witness for me.

"I don't know *who* you are now," Foss said, eyeing me as if he expected to face one of the aliens. "But when your trap springs shut, I promise you, we shall be ready to attend to you also!"

"Do we go back?" The other Patrolman stood by the tunnel door.

"I think not," Borton said. "I have no liking to be bottled up in there if we have to face trouble."

Foss had put my weapon inside his jacket. Now he made a sudden move behind me, caught my wrists before I was aware of what he planned to do. A moment later I found my hands secured behind my back. Even yet I could not believe that I had been so repudiated by my captain, that a Free Trader could turn on a crew member without allowing him a chance to defend himself.

"Which way?" he said in my ear as he tested my bonds. "Where are your friends waiting for us, Vorlund? But remember this—we have your Maelen. Serve us ill and you will never see her again. Or was your great concern for her only lip-deep and used as an excuse?"

"I know no more of what has happened than I have told you," I said, though I had no hope at all that he would believe me now. "The difference in the passages is as big a surprise to me as it is to you. There are old tales of tombs and treasures guarded by clever devices. Such a one could have been set here—perhaps this time defeated by our caps—"

"You expect us to believe that? When you told us that your very first explorations here brought you to a tomb, if tomb that hall was?" Foss's incredulity was plain.

"Why would I lead you into a trap, when I would also be caught in it?" I made a last try.

"Perhaps we have missed connections somewhere with the welcoming party," was Foss's answer. "Now—I asked you, Vorlund—which way?"

"I don't know."

The medic Thanel spoke up then. "That may be true. He could have been taken over, just as he said those others are. The cap might have broken that." He shrugged. "Take your choice of explanations."

"And choice of paths as well," Borton said. "Suppose we head right."

Borton and the Patrolman took the lead, Foss walked beside me, Thanel brought up the rear. The corridor was just wide enough for two of us to walk abreast. As was true elsewhere, there was breathable air introduced here by some

ingenious method of the constructors, though I never
sighted any duct by which it could enter. Underfoot there
was a thick carpet of dust which showed no disturbed marking—proof, I thought, that this was no traveled way.

The passage ended abruptly in a crossway in which were
set two doors, both closed. Our torches, shone directly on
them, displayed painted patterns there. Each I had seen
before, and perhaps I made some sound as I recognized
them. Foss spoke to me.

"This—you know it!" He made it an accusation rather
than a question.

What was clearly there in bold lines inlaid with strips of
metal (not painted as I had first thought) was the narrow
cat mask of the cliff. The slanted eyes of the creature were
gems which caught fire from our torches. The other door
bore the likeness of the crown of another alien—that which
resembled a prick-eared, long-muzzled animal.

"They are the signs of the alien crowns!"

Thanel had gone to the cat door, was running his hand
along the portal's outline.

"Locked, I would say. So do we use the laser on it?"

Borton made his own careful inspection. "Don't want to
set off any alarms. What about it, Vorlund? You're the
only one who knows this place. How do we open this?" He
looked to me as if this was some test of his own devising.

I was about to answer that I knew no more than he, when
Foss gave an exclamation. His hands went to the cap on his
head. He was not the only one to receive that jolt of force.
Thanel's lips twisted. He spoke slowly, one word at a time,
as if he were repeating some message to be relayed to the
rest of us.

"The—eyes—"

It was Borton, now standing closest to the panel, who cupped one palm over each of those glittering gems. I wanted to warn him off; my effort to cry out was a pain in my throat. But my only sound was a harsh croak.

I threw myself forward, struck the weight of my shoulder against his arm, striving to dislodge his hands. Then Foss's grip dragged me back in spite of my struggles.

There was a grating sound. Borton dropped his hands. The door was moving, lifting straight up. Then it stopped, leaving a space through which a man, stooping, might pass.

"Don't go in there!" Somehow I managed to uttter that warning. It was so plain to me, the aura of danger which spread from that hole like an invisible net to enfold us, that I could not understand why they did not also feel it. Too late; Borton had squeezed under the door, never glancing at me, his eyes so fixed on what lay ahead that he might be walking in a spell. After him went Thanel and the other Patrolman. Foss pushed me forward with a shove which was emphatic. I could not fight him.

So I passed under the barrier with every nerve alert to danger, knowing that I was a helpless prisoner facing a great peril I could not understand.

Chapter 15

KRIP VORLUND

I did not know what to expect, except that this place was so filled with a feeling of danger it might have been a monster's den. But what I saw looked far from dangerous, on the surface at least. I believe we were all a little dazed at the wonder of our find. The Throne of Qur, yes, that had been enough to incite cupidity as well as enchant the beholder. But that artifact was akin to a common bench in an inn compared to what was now gathered before us. Though I had not seen the temple treasures unpacked, still at that moment I was sure that all here outshone those.

There was a light which did not issue from our torches. And the contents of the chamber were not hidden from view in boxes and bundles, though there were two chests against the wall. The wall itself was inlaid with metal and stones. One section was formed of small, boxed scenes which gave one the illusion of gazing out through windows upon landscapes in miniature. I heard a sharp catch of breath from someone in our party. Then Borton advanced to the central picture.

That displayed a stretch of desert country. In the middle of the waste of sand arose a pyramid, shaped like those two rooms I had seen here. Save that this was out in the open, an erection of smoothed stone.

"That—that can't be!" The Patrol commander studied the scene as if he wanted someone to assure him that he did not view what his eyes reported. "It is impossible!"

I believed that he knew that building in the sand, that he had either seen it himself or viewed it on some tri-dee tape.

"It's—it's incredible!" Foss was not looking at the picture which had captured the commander's attention. Instead he gazed from one treasure to another as if he could not believe he was not dreaming.

As I have said, the contents of the room were all placed as if this chamber was in use as living quarters. The painted and inlaid chests stood against a wall on which those very realistic pictures were separated by hangings of colored stuffs, glowingly alive. Those possessed a surface shimmer so that one could not be sure, even when one stared at them, whether the odd rippling shadows which continually flickered and faded were indeed half-seen figures in action. Yet the strips hung motionless.

There were two high-backed chairs, one flanked by a small table which rested on a tripod of slender legs. Carved on the back of one chair was the cat mask, this time outlined in silver on a dead-black surface. The second chair was of a misty blue, bearing on its back a complicated design in pure white.

On the floor under our dusty boots lay a pattern of blocks, black as one chair, blue as the other, and inlaid with more symbols in silver. On the tripod table were small plates of crystal and a footed goblet.

Thanel crossed to the nearest chest. Catching his fingers under its projecting edge, he lifted, and the lid came up easily. We saw that the box was filled to the brim with lengths of color, green which was also blue, a warm yellow —perhaps garments. He did not take out any of them.

Chests, the two chairs, the table, and, directly facing the door, not another wall but a curtain of the same material as the wall panels. Foss started toward that and I followed close behind— *It* was beyond— He must not!

I was too late. He had already found the concealed slit which allowed one to pass through. I went closely on his heels, though I had already guessed what lay beyond. Guessed? No, *knew!*

And knowing, I expected to be met by a blast of the freezing air of stass-freeze— Come to think of it, why had we not already felt that in the outer chamber?

She lay with her head and shoulders supported by a thick cushion, gazing away from us, out through the crystal wall. But the tendrils of her crown swayed and entwined, moved, their cat-headed tips turning instantly, not only facing us, but making sharp jerking darts back and forth. It was as if those heads fought to detach the ties which held them to the circlet about the red hair, that they might come flying at us.

If she was not in freeze, then how had she been preserved? She could not be asleep, for her eyes were open. Nor could one detect even the slightest rise and fall of normal breathing.

"Thanel!" Foss went no farther in. At the sound of his

summons the cat heads spun and jerked, went into a wild
frenzy of action.

I was shoved aside as the medic joined us.

"Is—is she alive?" Foss demanded.

Thanel produced his life-force detect. Making some adjustments, he advanced. And it seemed to me he went
reluctantly, glancing now and then at the whirling crown.
He held the instrument up before the reclining woman,
studied its dial with a gathering frown, triggered some button, and once more took a reading.

"Well, is she?" Foss persisted.

"Not alive. But not dead either."

"And what does that mean?"

"Just what I said." Thanel pushed the button again with
the forefinger of his other hand. "It doesn't register either
way. And I don't know of any life force so alien that this
can't give an instant decision on the point. She isn't in
freeze, not in this atmosphere. But if she is dead I have
never seen such preservation before."

"Who is dead?" Borton came through the curtain now
with the other Patrolman, stopped short when he saw her.

I could no longer watch the woman. There was something in the constant motion of her cat-headed coronet
which disturbed me, as if those whirling thumb-sized bits of
metal wove a hypnotic spell. I made my last effort to warn
them.

"Dead or alive"—my voice was harsh, too loud in the
confinement of that room—"she reaches for you now. I tell
you—she is dangerous!"

Thanel looked at me. The others stood, their attention
all for her as if they had heard nothing. Then the medic

caught at the commander's arm, gave a sudden swift pull
which brought Borton around so he no longer eyed her
squarely. He blinked, swallowed as if he had gulped a
mouthful of some potent brew.

"Move!" The medic gave him a second push.

Borton, still blinking, stumbled back toward the curtain,
knocking against Foss. I was already on the other side of
the captain, had set my shoulder against his, using the
same tactics Thanel had, if in a more clumsy fashion. And
once shoved out of direct line with the woman, he, too,
seemed to wake.

In the end we all got back on the other side of the curtain and stood there, breathing a little heavily, almost as if
we had been racing. I was aware that the cap on my head
was warm, that the line of wire touching my temples was
near burning me. I saw Thanel touch his own band, snatch
his fingers away. But Foss was at my side.

"Turn around."

I obeyed his order, felt him busy at my wrists. A moment
later my hands were free.

"I can believe," he said, "in anything happening here,
Vorlund. After seeing that, I can believe! She is just as you
described her. And I believe she is deadly!"

"What about the others?" Thanel asked.

"There is one there." I rubbed my left wrist with my
right hand, nodding in the direction where the next compartment must lie. "Two more on the other two sides. One
held Griss when I was here before."

Borton went again to that picture of the pyramid. "Do
you know what this is?"

"No. But it is plain to guess you have seen its like before,

and not on Sekhmet," Foss returned. "Does it have any
importance for us now?"

"Perhaps. That—that was built on Terra in a past so
distant we can no longer reckon it accurately. By accounts
the archaeologists have never agreed on its age. It is supposed to have been erected by slave labor at a time when
man had not yet tamed a beast of burden, had not discovered the wheel. And yet it was a great feat of highly
sophisticated engineering. There were countless theories
about it, one being that its measurements, because of their
unusual accuracy, held a message. It was not the only such
either, but one of several. Though this particular one was
supposed to be the first and greatest. For a long time the
pile was said to be the tomb of a ruler. But that theory was
never entirely proved—for the tomb itself might have been
a later addition. At any rate, it was built millennia before
our breed took to space!"

"But Forerunner remains," Thanel objected. "Those
were never found on Terra. None of the history tapes
records such discoveries."

"Perhaps no remains recognized as such by us. But—"
Borton shook his head. "What do we even know of Terra
now except from tapes copied and recopied, some of them
near-legendary? Yet—and this is also very odd indeed—in
the land where that stood"—he pointed to the picture—
"they once worshiped gods portrayed with human bodies
and beast or bird heads. In fact—there was a cat-headed
goddess Sekhmet, a bird-headed Thoth, a saurian Set—"

"But these planets, this system, were named by the First-
in Scout who mapped them, after the old custom of naming
systems for ancient gods!" Foss interrupted.

"That is true. The Scouts gave such names as suited their fancies—culled from the tapes they carried with them to relieve the boredom of spacing. And the man who named this system must have had a liking for Terran history. Yet —he could also have been influenced in some way." Borton again shook his head. "We may never know the truth of the past, save this is such a find as may touch on very ancient mysteries, even those of our own beginnings!"

"And we may not have a chance to learn anything, unless we get to the bottom of a few modern mysteries now!" Foss retorted.

I noted that he kept his head turned away from the curtain, almost as if she who waited beyond it might have the power to pull him back into her presence. The wires of my cap no longer were heated; but I was unhappy in this place, I wanted out.

"That crown she wears—" Thanel shifted from one foot to another as if he wanted to look at the woman again. I saw Borton shake his head. "I would say it is a highly sensitive communication device of some sort. What about it, Laird?"

"Undoubtedly—" began the other Patrolman. "Didn't you feel the response of your protect? The caps were close to shorting, holding against that energy. What about the crowns the others wear?" He turned to me. "Are they alive —moving—also?"

"Not that I saw. They aren't shaped the same."

"I want to see the alien body holding Griss," Foss broke in. "Is that in the next chamber?"

I shook my head. And I had no idea of how one reached

either the interior of the crystal-lined pyramid room or the
other chambers which formed its walls. There had been
another door beside the cat one. But side by side—when
the rooms were at right angles—how—

Foss did not wait for my guidance. He slipped under the
outer door and we were quick to follow. Thanel brought
down the cat door, it moving much more easily to close
than it had to open. Foss was already at work on the other
door. It yielded as reluctantly as the first had done, but it
did go up. However, we did not look now on a room filled
with treasures, but on a very narrow passage, so confined
one had to turn sideways to slip along it. This made a
right-angled turn and then there was a second curtained
doorway ahead.

"This one?" Foss demanded.

"No." I tried to remember. "Next, I think."

We slipped along that slit between walls to a second
sharp turn, which brought us so that we must now be facing directly across from the chamber of the cat woman, if
we could have seen through solid walls. Once more there
was a door, this one patterned with the bird head. A third
turn and we found what I had been searching for—the
saurian.

"This is it!"

The door panel was doubly hard to dislodge because there
was so little room in which to move. However, it gave at
last, Foss and I working at it as best we could.

Once more we were in a furnished room. But we spent
no time in surveying the treasures there, hurrying on instead
through the curtain to the fore part. I could see now the

crowned head, the bare shoulders of him who sat there, staring stonily out into the space beyond the crystal.

Foss circled to be able to see the face of the seated one. There was no moving part of this crown, no stirring to suggest that we had found more than a perfectly preserved alien body. But I saw the captain's expression change, knew that he could read the eyes in that set face and felt the same horror I had felt.

"Griss!" His whisper was a hiss.

I did not want to view what Foss now faced with grim determination, yet I knew that I must. So I edged forward on the other side of the chair, looked into the tortured eyes. Griss—yes—and still conscious, still aware of what had happened to him! Though I had passed through body change twice, both times it had been with my own consent and for a good purpose. However, had such a change been wrought against my will—could I have kept such knowledge and remained sane? I did not know.

"We have to do something!" The words exploded from Foss with the force of a blaster shot. I knew that he backed them with that determination which he had ever shown in the face of any peril that threatened the *Lydis* and those who called her their home. "You"—he spoke directly to me—"have tried this body exchange. What can you do for him?"

Always in such matters I had been the passive one, the one who was worked upon, not the mover in the act. Maelen had sung me into the barsk body when the Three Rings of Sotrath wreathed that moon over our heads, when the occult powers of the Thassa were at their greatest height.

And I had passed into the shell of Maquad in the shelter of Umphra, where the priests of that gentle and protective order had been able to lend to Maelen all the aid she needed.

Once only had I seen the transfer for another—that in a time of fear and sorrow when Maelen had lain dying and one of her little people, Vors, had crept to her side and offered her furred body as a refuge for the Thassa spirit. I had seen them sing the exchange then, two of the Thassa, Maelen's sister and her kinsman. And I had found myself also singing words I did not know. But that I alone could make such an exchange—no.

"I can do—" I was about to add "nothing" when a thought came from my own past. I had run as Jorth the barsk; I now walked as Maquad. Could it just be— If Griss tried, overcame his horror and fear of what had happened to him, could he command this new body, rule it until he could recapture his own? But I must get through to him first. And that would mean setting aside the protect cap.

I explained, not quite sure whether this could be done, even if I dared so break our own defenses and put us all in danger. But when I had made this clear Foss touched the butt of the laser.

"We have our defenses. You know what I mean—will you risk that also?"

Be burned down if I were taken over—no, I did not want to risk that, but want and a man's duty are two different things many times during one's life. I had turned aside from what the Traders considered my duty once already, here on Sekhmet. It seemed that now I had a second chance to repay old debts. And I remembered how Maelen had faced exile in an alien body because she had taken up a debt.

"It may be his only chance."

Quickly, before I could falter, I reached for the cap on my head. I saw them move to encircle me, weapons ready. They all eyed me warily as if I were now the enemy. I took off the cap.

My head felt light, free, as if I had removed some burden which had weighed heavily without my even being aware of it. I had a moment of hesitation, as one might feel stepping out into an arena such as those on Sparta where men face beasts in combat. From which direction could an attack come? And I believe those around me waited tensely for some hideous change in me.

"Griss?" The impression that time was limited set me directly to work. "Griss!" I was not a close comrade of this poor prisoner. But we were shipmates; we had drawn matching watch buttons many times, shared planet leaves. It had been through him I had first learned who and what Maelen was. And now I consciously drew upon that friendship of the past to buttress my sending.

"Griss!" And this time—

"Krip—can you—can you hear me?" Incredulous thankfulness.

"Yes." I came directly to the importance of what must be done. "Griss, can you rule this body? Make it obey you?" The question was the best way I knew of trying to make him break down a barrier which might have been built by his own fears. Now he must try to direct the alien husk, even as a control board directs a labor robo.

I had had a hard time adjusting to an animal form; at
least he did not have to face that. For the alien, to our
eyes, was humanoid.

"Can you rule the body, Griss?"

His surprise was easy to read. I knew that he had not
considered that at all, that the initial horror of what had
happened to him had made him believe himself helpless
from the first. Whereas I had been helped through my
transitions by foreknowledge, and also by the aid of Maelen,
who was well versed in such changes, he had been brutally
taken prisoner in such a way as to paralyze even his thought
processes for a time. It is always the unknown which carries
with it, especially for my species, the greatest fear.

"Can I?" he asked as might a child.

"Try—concentrate!" I ordered him with authority. "Your
hand—your right hand, Griss. Raise it—order it to move!"

His hands rested on the arms of the chair in which he
sat. His head did not move a fraction, but his eyes shifted
away from mine, in a visible effort to see his hands.

"Move it!"

The effort he unleashed was great. I hastened to feed
that. Fingers twitched—

"Move!"

The hand rose, shaking as if it had been so long inert
that muscles, bone, flesh could hardly obey the will of the
brain. But it rose, moved a little away from the support
of the chair arm, then wavered, fell limply upon the knee.
But he had moved it!

"I—I did it! But—weak—very—weak—"

I looked to Thanel. "The body may be in need of restor-
atives—perhaps as when coming out of freeze."

He frowned. "No equipment for that type of restoration."

"But you must have something in your field kit—some kind of basic energy shot."

"Alien metabolism," he murmured, but he brought out his field kit, unsealed it. "We can't tell how the body will react."

"Tell him—" Griss's thought was frantic. "Try anything! Better be dead than like this!"

"You are far from dead," I countered.

Thanel held an injection cube, still in its sterile envelope. He bent over the seated body to affix the cube on the bare chest over the spot where a human heart would have been. At least it did adhere, was not rejected at once.

That body gave a jerk as visible shudders ran along the limbs.

"Griss?"

"Ahhh—" No message, just a transferred sensation of pain, of fear. Had Thanel been right and the restorative designed for our species proved dangerous to another?

"Griss!" I caught at that hand he had moved with such effort, held it between both of mine. Only my tight grasp kept it from flailing out in sharp spasms. The other had snapped up from the chair arm, waved in the air. The legs kicked out; the body itself writhed, as if trying to rise and yet unable to complete such movement.

Now that frozen, expressionless face came alive. The mouth opened and shut as if he screamed, though no sound came from his lips. Those lips themselves drew back, flattened in the snarl of a cornered beast.

"It's killing him!" Foss put out a hand as if to knock that cube away, but the medic caught his wrist.

"Let it alone! To interrupt now *will* kill."

I had captured the other hand, held them both as I struggled to reach the mind behind that tortured face.

"Griss!"

He did not answer. However, his spasms were growing less; his face was no longer so contorted. I did not know if that was a good or a bad sign.

"Griss?"

"I—am—here—" The thought-answer was so slow it came like badly slurred speech. "I—am—still—here—"

I detected a dull wonder in his answer, as if he were surprised to find it so.

"Griss, can you use your hands?" I released the grip with which I had held them, laid them back on his knees.

They no longer shook nor waved about. Slowly they rose until they were chest-high before him. The fingers balled into fists, straightened out again, wriggled one after another as if they were being tested.

"I can!" The lethargy of his answer of only moments earlier was gone. "Let me—let me up!"

Those hands went to the arms of the chair. I could see the effort which he expended to use them to support him to his feet. Then he made it, stood erect, though he wavered, kept hold of the chair. Thanel was quickly at one side, I at the other, supporting him. He took several uncertain steps, but those grew firmer.

The restorative cube, having expended its charge, loosened and fell from his chest, which arched and fell now as he drew deep breaths into his lungs. Again I had reason to admire the fine development of this body. It was truly as if some idealized sculpture of the human form had come to life. He was a good double palms' space taller than either of us who walked with him, and muscles moved more and more easily under his pale skin.

"Let me try it alone." He did not mind-speak now, but aloud. There was a curious flatness to his tone, a slight hesitation, but we had no difficulty in understanding him. And we released our hold, though we stood ready if there was need.

He went back and forth, his strides sure and balanced now. And then he paused by the chair, put both his hands to his head, and took off that grotesque crown, dropping it to clang on the seat as he threw it away.

His bared skull was hairless, like that of the body in the freeze box. But he ran his hands back and forth across the skin there as if he wanted to reassure himself that the crown was gone.

"I did it!" There was triumph in that. "Just as you thought I could, Krip. And if I can—they can too!"

Chapter 16

KRIP VORLUND

"Who are *they*?" Foss asked.

"Lidj—the Patrol officer—there and there!" He faced the outer transparent wall of the room, pointed right and left to those other two aliens on display. "I saw them—saw them being brought in, forced to exchange. Just as was done with me!"

"I wonder why such exchanges are necessary," Thanel said. "If we could restore this body, why didn't they just restore their own? Why go through the business of taking over others?"

Griss was rubbing his forehead with one hand. "Sometimes—sometimes I know things—things they knew. I think they value their bodies too highly to risk them."

"Part of their treasures!" Foss laughed harshly. "Use someone else to do their work for them, making sure they have a body to return to if that substitute suffers any harm. They're as cold-blooded as harpy night demons! Well, let's see if we can get Lidj and that man of yours out of pawn now."

Borton leaned over the edge of the chair, reaching for the crown Griss had thrown there.

"No!" In a stride Griss closed the distance between them, sent the crown spinning across the floor. "In some way that is a com, giving them knowledge of what happens to the body—"

"Then, with your breaking that tie," I pointed out, "they —or he—will be suspicious and come looking—"

"Better that than have him force me under control again without my knowing when that might happen!" Griss retorted.

If the danger he seemed to believe in did exist, he was right. And we might have very little time.

Borton spoke first. "All the more reason to try to get the others free."

"Which one is Lidj?" Foss was already going.

"To the left."

That meant the bird-headed crown. We returned to the anteroom. Griss threw open one of the chests as if he knew exactly what he was looking for. He dragged out a folded bundle and shook it out, to pull on over his bare body a tightly fitting suit of dull black. It was all of a piece including footgear, even gloves, rolled back now about the wrists, and a hood which hung loose between the shoulders. A press of finger tip sealed openings, leaving no sign they had ever existed.

There was something odd about that garment. The dull black seemed to produce a visual fuzziness, so that only his head and bared hands were well-defined. It must have been an optical illusion, but I believed that with gloves and hood on he might be difficult to see.

"How did you know where to find that?" Borton was watching him closely.

Griss, who had been sealing the last opening of his clothing, stopped, his finger tip still resting on the seam. There was a shadow of surprise on his handsome face.

"I don't know—I just knew that it was there and I must wear it."

Among them all, I understood. This was the old phenomenon of shape-changing—the residue (hopefully the very *small* residue) of the earlier personality taking over for some actions. But there was danger in that residue. I wondered if Griss knew that, or if we would have to watch him ourselves lest he revert to the alien in some more meaningful way.

Thanel must have been thinking along the same lines, for now he demanded: "How much do you remember of alien ways?"

Griss's surprise was tinged with uneasiness.

"Nothing! I was not even thinking—just that I needed clothing. Then I knew where to find it. It—I just knew— that's all!"

"How much else would he 'just know,' I wonder?" Borton looked to Thanel rather than to Griss, as if he expected a better explanation from the medic.

"Wasting time!" Foss stood by the door. "We have to get Lidj and Harkon! And get out before anyone comes to see what happened to Griss."

"What about my cap?" I asked.

Thanel had passed that to the other Patrolman. And in this place I wanted all the protection I could get. The other held it out to me and I settled it on my head with a sigh of relief, though with it came the sensation of an oppressive burden.

We threaded along that very narrow passage to the next chamber, where the alien with the avian crown half-reclined on the couch. Having freed one "exchange" prisoner, I now moved with confidence. And it was not so difficult, as Juhel Lidj had greater esper power.

Then we retraced our way and released Harkon also. But I do not believe that Borton was entirely happy over such additions to our small force. They had put aside their crowns, and they were manifestly eager to move against those who had taken their bodies. But whether they would stand firm during a confrontation, we could not know.

We returned to the cat door. There I lingered a moment, studying the mask symbol. Three men, one woman—who had they been? Rulers; priests and a priestess; scientists of another time and place? Why had they been left here? Was this a depository like our medical freezers, or a politically motivated safe-keep where rulers had chosen to wait out some revolution they had good reason to fear? Or—

It seemed to me that the gem eyes of the cat held a malicious glitter, mirroring superior amusement. As if someone knew exactly the extent of my ignorance and dismissed me from serious consideration because of it. A spark of anger flared deep inside me. Yet I did not underrate what lay beyond that door and could be only waiting for a chance to assume power.

"Now where?" Borton glanced about as if he expected some guide sign to flare into life.

"Our other men," Lidj answered that crisply. "They have them imprisoned somewhere—"

I thought that "somewhere" within these burrows was
no guide at all. And it would seem Foss's thoughts marched
with mine, for he asked:

"You have no idea where?"

It was Harkon who answered. "Not where they are.
Where *our* bodies are now, that is something else."

"You mean you can trace those?" Thanel demanded.

"Yes. Though whether mere confrontation will bring
about another exchange—"

"How do you know?" The medic pursued the first part
of his answer.

"I can't tell you. Frankly, I don't know. But I do know
that whoever is walking about as Harkon right now is in
that direction." There was no hesitation as he pointed to
the right wall of the passage.

Only, not being able to ooze through solid rock, I did
not see how that knowledge was going to benefit us. We
had found no other passage during our way in (I was still
deeply puzzled about the difference between my first venture into the maze and this one).

Harkon still faced that blank wall, a frown on his face.
He stared so intently at the smoothed stone that one might
well think he saw a pattern there—one invisible to us.

After a moment he shook his head. "Not quite here—
farther on," he muttered. Nor did he enlarge on that, but
started along close to the wall, now and then sweeping his
finger tips across it, as if by touch he might locate what he
could not find by sight. He was so intent upon that search
that his concentration drew us along, though I did not
expect any results from his quest. Then he halted, brought
the palm of his hand against the stone in a hard slap.

"Right behind here—if we can break through."

"Stand aside." Whether Borton accepted him as a guide or not, the commander seemed willing to put it to the test. He aimed his weapon at the wall where Harkon had indicated, and fired.

The force of that weapon was awesome, more so perhaps because we were in such a confined space. One moment there had been the solid rock of this planet's bone; the next —a dark hole. Before we could stop him, Harkon was into that.

We had indeed broken through into another corridor. This one was washed in gray light. Harkon did not hesitate, but moved along with such swift strides that we had to hurry to catch up.

That passage was short, for we soon came out on a gallery running along near the top of another pyramid-shaped chamber. This one was triple the size of the others I had seen. From our perch we looked down into a scene of clanking activity. There was a mass of machinery, installations of some sort, being uncrated, unboxed by robos. Pieces were lifted by raise cranes, transferred to transports. But those carriers ran neither on wheels nor—

"Antigrav!" Borton leaned nearer to the edge. "They have antigrav in small mobile units."

Antigrav we knew. But the principle could not be used in mobile units, only installed in buildings as a method of transport from floor to floor. Here these carriers, loaded with heavy burdens, swung along in ordered lines through a dark archway in the opposite wall.

"Where's the controller?" The other Patrolman peered over.

"Remote control, I would say." Foss stood up.

We had all fallen flat at the sign of the activity. But now Foss apparently thought we had nothing to fear. And a moment later he added:

"Those are programmed robos."

Programmed robos! The complexity of the operation here on Sekhmet increased with every discovery we made. Programmed robos were not ordinarily ship workers, like the controlled ones we had earlier seen and used ourselves. They were far more intricate, requiring careful servicing, which made them impractical for use on primitive worlds. One did not find them on the frontier. Yet here they were at work light-years away from the civilizations producing them. Shipping these here, preparing them for work, would have been a major task in itself.

"In a jack hideout?" Foss protested.

"Look closer!" Borton was still watching below. "This is is a storehouse which is being systematically looted. And who would have situated it here in the first place—"

"Forerunners," Lidj answered him. "But machines—this is not a tomb, nor—"

"Nor a lot of things!" Borton interrupted. "There were Forerunner installations found on Limbo. The only difference is that those were abandoned, not stored away. Here —perhaps a whole civilization was kept—both men and machines! And the Forerunners were not a single civilization, either—even a single species. Ask the Zacathans—they can count you off evidence of perhaps ten which have been tentatively identified, plus fragments of other, earlier ones which have not! The universe is a graveyard of vanished races, some of whom rose to heights we cannot assess today.

These machines, if they can be made to work again, their purposes learned—"

I think that the possibilities of what he said awed us. Of course, we all knew of such treasure hunting as had been indulged in on Thoth—that was common. Lucky finds had been made all around the galaxy from time to time. The Zacathans, that immensely old, immensely learned reptilian race whose passion was the accumulation of knowledge, had their libraries filled with the lore of vanished—long-vanished—stellar civilizations. They led their archaeological expeditions from world to world seeking a treasure they reckoned not in the furnishings of tombs, in the hidden hoards discovered in long-deserted ruins, but in the learning of those who had left such links with the far past.

And parties of men had made such finds also. They had spoken of Limbo—that had been the startling discovery of a Free Trader in the earlier days.

Yet the plunder from here had not yet turned up on any inner-planet market, where it would logically be sold. Its uniqueness would have been recognized instantly, for rumor of such finds spreads quickly and far.

"Suppose"—Foss, plainly fascinated, still watched the antigravs floating in parade order out of the storeroom— "the jacks, even the Guild, began this. But now it has been taken over by those others."

"Yes," came the dry, clipped answer from Lidj. "It could be that the original owners are now running the game." He raised both hands to his bald skull, rubbed his fingers across it. There was still a mark on his forehead from the weight of the crown.

"You mean—" Borton began.

Lidj turned on him. "Is that so strange? We put men in stass-freeze for years. In fact I do not know what has been the longest freeze time ending in a successful resuscitation. These might be awakened to begin life at the point where they left off, ready for their own plan of action. Do you deny that they have already proved they have secrets which we have not? Ask your own man, Harkon—how can he explain what has happened to the three of us?"

"But the others stored here—at least that one in the box above the valley—was dead." My protest was weak, because too much evidence was on Lidj's side.

"Perhaps most of them did die, perhaps that is why they want our bodies. Who knows? But I will wager that they— those three who took ours—are now in command of this operation!"

Harkon had drawn a little apart, perilously close to the edge of the balcony. Now he spoke in the same husky tone our cargomaster used.

"Can you set an interrupt beam on these lasers you have?" I did not understand what he meant, but apparently his question made sense to Borton, who joined him.

"Tricky—from here," the commander observed.

"Tricky or not, we can try it. Let me see yours—"

Did Borton hesitate for a moment before he passed over that weapon? If so, I could understand, since lurking at the back of my mind was a shadowy suspicion of these three. It is never easy to accept body exchange, even for one knowing the Thassa.

But Borton appeared willing to trust the pilot and passed over the laser. Harkon squatted against the sharply sloping wall, which made him hunch over the weapon. He snapped open the charge chamber, inspected the cartridge there, closed it once more, and reset the firing dial.

With it in his hand he went to peer down, selecting a victim. There was a robo to his left, now engaged in shifting a metal container onto one of the waiting transports. Harkon took aim and pressed the firing button.

A crackle of lightning sped like a whiplash, not to touch the robo itself, but to encircle its knoblike head. The robo had a flexible tentacle coiled about the container, ready to swing it across to the platform. But that move was never completed. The robo froze with the container still in the air.

"By the Teeth of Stanton Gore, you did it!" Borton's voice was almost shrill.

The pilot wasted no time in waiting for congratulations on his skill. He had already aimed at the next robo and stopped that one dead also.

"So you can knock them out," Lidj observed. "What do we do now—" Then he paused and caught at Borton's arm. "Is there a chance of resetting them?"

"We can hope so."

The robos I knew and had always used were control ones. Free Traders visited only the more backward worlds where machines were simple if used at all. I had no idea how one went about reprogramming complex robos. But the knowledge of a Free Trader was not that of a Patrolman. Plainly Borton and Harkon hoped the machines could be made to work in some manner for us.

Which is what they proceeded to find out. When the six robos were halted we came down from the balcony. The antigrav transports still moved at a slow and even pace, though those now edging away were only partly loaded.

Foss and the other Patrolman went into action, turning
their lasers with less precision but as great effect on the
motive section of those. The carriers crashed to the floor
with heavy jars which shook even this rock-walled chamber.

The Patrolmen gathered about the nearest robo. Harkon
was already at work on the protective casing over its "brain."
But I was more interested in the transports. Basically these
were nothing more than ovals of metal, with low side walls
to hold their loads in place. The motive force of each lay in
a box at the rear. The principle of their construction was
unlike anything I had ever seen before.

"Something coming!" At that warning from Griss we all
went to ground. But what loomed into view out of the
opening was an empty transport back for another load. Foss
had raised his laser to short it when Lidj jerked at his arm
to spoil his aim.

"We can use that!" He made a running jump, caught the
edge of the carrier's wall, and swung up on it. It did not
halt its forward movement, proceeding steadily down a row
of boxes until it came to a stop beside a motionless robo,
still holding a crate aloft between clawed appendages.

Lidj was squatting before the controls, trying to make
sense of them, when we clambered on board to join him.
Unloaded as it was, the carrier bucked a little under our
movements and shifting weight, so we had to take care.

"Could be set either of two ways," he said, "ready to go
either when there is a certain amount of weight on board—
or after a predetermined time. If it is the latter it's more
risky. We'll have to either knock it out or let it go. But if
it is a matter of weight—"

Foss nodded. "Then we can use it."

I could guess what they planned. Build a row of boxes around the edge of the carrier, then take our places inside that and have transportation out without fear of getting lost. We would, of course, be heading toward the enemy. But we would have the element of surprise on our side.

"Time it," Foss continued.

I looked around. A second empty carrier was now coming in, heading, not to where we waited, but to the loading site, where the Patrolmen now had the upper casing of the robo free.

"Look out!"

Those workmen scattered as the carrier swung in, just missing the upraised load arm of the robo. Then the platform halted, waiting to be loaded. The men arose to tug at the squat robo, pulling it out of the way to where they could get at it without any danger of being knocked out by a transport.

Lidj still knelt by the motive box. He had stopped trying to find any lever or control button. Foss had said to time it, and we were all counting furiously during long minutes as we stood tensely alert for the first sign that the carrier was preparing to move. But it hung there, still waiting. I heard the captain's sigh of relief.

"One hundred," he repeated aloud. "If it doesn't start up by five, now—"

His lips shaped the numbers visibly. The carrier did not stir.

"So far, so good. Weight must be what triggers it."

While we had conducted our crude test a third carrier had come nosing back. Counting the three which had been immobilized, there were now six. How many could there be in all? And how soon would someone come looking if they did not return?

Foss and Lidj went to one of the loaded ones which had been halted. Part of a cargomaster's duty is the judging of cargo loads, an ability to estimate, by eye, bulk and weight for stowage. Lidj was an expert. I was not so experienced, but I had had enough general training under his stiff tutelage to be able to come close to guessing the weight load on the downed platform.

Once we knew that, we moved along the still-racked boxes to pick out those which would give us protective bulk without too much weight—weight which our bodies must partly supply.

Having made our choices, we began to load by hand, a wearying process which was foreign to usual ship work. But in times of stress one can do many things he might earlier have thought impossible. We stacked our chosen boxes and containers as a bulwark running along the edges of the platform, leaving an open space between. Borton came to inspect our labors and nodded approval.

"Just let us get one of those boys going"—he nodded to the robos—"and we'll move out."

What he intended the reprogrammed cargo handler to do, I could not guess. Nor did we take time from our own labor to watch their struggles. There came a whir of sound. The robo brought down its upright arm, dropped the box it held. It turned on its treads to face the wide doorway.

"Now—" Harkon was moving to a second robo as if he planned to use that also. Then his hands went to his head.

"Time's just run out." His voice lacked the jubilation of seconds earlier. "If we make a move—it must be now!"

Chapter 17

KRIP VORLUND

No other carrier had returned for some time now. But Griss, Lidj, and Harkon all faced the doorway as if they heard some call.

"They are uneasy, those who wear our bodies," Harkon said to Borton. "We shall have to move fast if we would keep any advantage."

Borton triggered the robo and it moved out, heading for the door. With it as a fore guard, the rest of us took to the carriers. And as those edged away from the loading sites, picking up speed as they went, I could have shouted aloud in my relief. Our calculations had been proved right so far. Weight sent the carriers on their way.

Once airborne, I longed for the speed of a flitter. But there was no hurrying the deliberate pace, any more than we could urge on the robo rumbling ahead. Perhaps it was just as well we did not approach too near that. For as it went it came alive. It had been using two long, jointed

arms, ending in clawed attachments. And it was also
equipped with flexible tentacles, two above and two below
those arms. Now all six of the appendages flailed the air
vigorously, whipping out and around.

Though men have depended upon the services of machines for such countless ages that perhaps only the
Zacathans can now reckon the number of those dusty years,
yet I think deep inside us all there lingers a small spark of
fear that some day, under some circumstances, those
machines will turn on us, to wreak a mindless vengeance of
their own. Long ago it was discovered that robos given too
human a look were not salable. Even faint resemblances
triggered such age-old distaste.

Now as I lay beside Foss and Lidj on the carrier and
watched the wildly working arms of the robo, which seemed
to have gone mad, I was glad that ours was not the first
transport riding directly in its wake, but the second. Let
the Patrol enjoy—if one might term it that—the honor of
the lead. The farther I was from that metal monster seemingly intent on smashing the world, the better.

"They are not too far ahead now." Lidj's words reached
me through the *clank-clank* of the robo.

"How many?" Foss wanted to know.

"My powers are not that selective; sorry." There was the
ghost of Lidj's old dry humor in that answer. "I just know
that my body is somewhere ahead. My body! Tell me, Krip"
—he looked to me then—"did you ever stand off and watch
yourself, back there on Yiktor?"

I remembered—though then the transition had been so
great, my own adaptation to an animal's body had put such

a strain on me, that I had been far more concerned with
my own feelings at the moment than with what was happening to the body I had discarded.

"Yes, but not for long. Those men of Osokun's took me
—it—away. And at the time I was, well, I was learning
what it meant to be a barsk."

"At least we did not have that factor. It is hard enough
to adapt to this covering," Lidj commented. "In fact, I
must admit it has a few advantages over my own. Several
aches and pains have been eliminated. Not that I care to
remain in my present tenancy any longer than I have to. I
fear I am conservative in such matters."

I marveled at what seemed my superior's almost compla-
cent acceptance of a situation which might have unseated
the reason of a less self-controlled man.

"I hope," he continued, "that the one wearing *me* has
no heroic tendencies. Getting my body smashed up before
I can retrieve it would be a disappointment—to say the
least!"

With that he resurrected my own worries. Maelen—her
present body could not continue to live, not long, if we
roused her from freeze. And could it last, even in that state,
long enough to get her back to Yiktor? How— I tried to
think of ways that journey could be accomplished safely,
only to reject each idea, knowing all were such wild plans
as could be dreamed by graz chewers, and as likely to be
realized.

The light ahead was brighter. Now the robo clanked on
into the source of that, the first of our carriers closely behind him, ours drawn after without our guidance. We had
our weapons and the protection of the bulwarks we had

built about the edges of the platforms. Though those now
seemed very thin shells indeed.

Here were piles of goods out of the storage place. And
moving among them were the common controlled robos,
sorting and transporting to a cargo hoist which dangled
from the hatch of a ship. A single glance told me that we
were in that landing valley and that this was the same ship
Maelen and I had seen when we fled the burrows. How
long ago had that been? We had eaten E rations, gulped
down sustain pills until I was no longer sure of time. A
man can exist long on such boosters without even being
aware that he must rest.

Our carriers kept on at the same even pace, but the robo
was not so orderly. Its path was straight ahead, and it did
not try to avoid anything in its path. The whiplash of its
tentacles, the battery of its arms crashed into the cargo
awaiting stowage, sweeping away battered and broken
boxes, some to be crushed beneath its own massive treads.

The surprise was complete. I heard shouting—saw the
lightning fire of lasers, bringing down more of the cargo,
melting some of it. And the shock of those energy waves
did their work. Men toppled, to lie clawing feebly at the
ground, their minds knocked out for a space by the back
fire of such force. We tumbled from our transports, took
to cover among the cargo.

Producing tanglers, the Patrolmen moved in toward those
feebly moving jacks while we slipped ahead, searching for
more humans among the working robos. The reprogrammed
one smashed on and on until it came up with a crash
against one of the ship's fins. There it continued to whir
sullenly, not backing away, unable to move on. An arm

caught in the dangling chains of the hoist. Having so con-
nected, it tightened hold with a vicious snap. Before whoever was running the crane could shut it off, the robo had
been lifted a little. Then the strain of its weight told, broke
the hoist chain. That small shift of position had been
enough to pull the robo away from the fin. Dropped to the
ground again, it still moved—though its assault on the fin
had damaged it, and it proceeded with an ear-punishing
grating noise. One of its arms hung limply down, jangling
back and forth against its outer casing; the other clutched
and tore with as much vigor as ever as it rumbled on the
new course.

I saw Lidj as I rounded a stack of boxes. He was heading,
not toward the scene of action, but away from it, crouching
low as if he expected blaster fire. And there was that in his
attitude which drew me after him. A moment later Harkon
closed in from the left, his black suit conspicuous here in
the open. Then came another dark figure—Griss. They were
running, dodging, their empty hands held a little before
them in an odd fashion, with the fingers arched, resembling
the claws of the robo still engaged in senseless destruction
near the ship. And they did not look right or left, but
directly before them, as if their goal was in plain sight.

Watching them, I knew a rise of old fear. It could be
that they were again under the command of those aliens
who had taken over their bodies. And it might be better
now for all of us were I to use the side wash of my laser to
knock them out.

I was beginning to aim when Griss shot forward in a
spring, launching himself into the mouth of the cavern
where the jack camp was. By that leap he barely avoided a

burst of greenish light. Another of those bursts flowered
where Harkon had half-crouched as he ran—but the pilot
was no longer there. His reactions were quicker than
human. It was almost as if he sensed danger and his fear
brought about instant teleportation. Yet I saw him only a
little beyond where that green bubble had burst.

That the aliens must be in there was plain. I did not
have the same agility which the three ahead of me possessed; yet I followed. What a meeting between the three
and their alien enemies would bring about, no one could
tell. It might well be that confronting them would reduce
our men to puppets. If that were so—well, I held a laser
and knew what to do.

But, try my best, I could not keep up with the three. I did
see them by the plasta-bubble. The piles of loot had been
much reduced since I had last seen them—there was not
enough left to provide much cover. But the three were not
trying for any concealment now. Instead they had drawn
together, Harkon in the center, my two shipmates flanking
him. Were they under control? I could not tell and, until
I was certain, I must not venture too close. I lurked in the
shadows by the entrance, berating myself for my own indecision.

Those whom the three sought were there, back in the
greater gloom under the overhang of the balcony where I
had once been trapped by him who wore Griss's body.
Lidj, Harkon, Griss—yet they were not the men I knew.
Those were the three apparent aliens advancing toward
them. There were others there also, those with whom I
had begun that scouting patrol, the men from the *Lydis*
and the Patrol.

They were ranged against the wall, standing very still, staring straight ahead, no sign of emotion on their set faces. There was a robo-like quality to their waiting. Nor were they alone. Other men, jacks probably, were drawn up flanking them. All were armed, blasters ready in their hands, as if their alien leaders had nothing to fear from any revolt on their part.

Yet they did not aim at the three advancing. Slowly that advance faltered. The black-clad alien bodies came to a stop. Wearing the protect cap, I received only a faint backwash of the struggle in progress. But that the aliens were striving for control over their bodies was plain.

Of the three, Griss was the first to turn about and face outward, his expression now as blank as those of the men under alien domination. Then Harkon—and Lidj. With the same uniformity with which they had entered the cavern, they began to march out, and behind them the rest of the controlled company followed.

Perhaps the aliens thought to use them as a screen, a way of reaching us. But if they did so, they were not of the type who lead their own armies, for they themselves did not stir away from the wall.

Had I waited too long? Could I use the laser with the necessary accuracy the Patrolmen had shown? In any case even death, I believed, would be more welcome to those I saw under control than the life to which these others had condemned them.

I sighted over the heads of the three at the fore and fired.

The crackle of the released energy was twice as spectacular here. Or else I had not judged well and set the discharge too high. But those over whose heads it passed cried out,

loosed their weapons, staggered, and went down. The three
at the van marched on a step or two, and I thought I must
have failed to knock them out, save that their strength
did not hold for long and they wilted, going to their knees,
then lying prone. Yet their outstretched hands scrabbled
on the floor as if they still sought to drag their bodies on.

At the same time that backwash of compulsion I had
felt, even when wearing the cap, strengthened. The enemy
did not have to seek me out! They knew where I was as well
as if I stood in the open shouting for their attention. But
it was by my will alone that I came out of cover, walking
through the prone ranks of their stricken attack force to
face them.

Their arrogance, their supreme confidence in themselves
and their powers, was not betrayed in any expression on
the three faces which I knew well but which now wore a
veil of strangeness, as if the Terran features formed a mask
for the unknown. No, their belief in themselves and their
powers was an almost tangible aura about them.

Still I did not surrender as they willed me to. Or perhaps
they were striving to launch me, as they had those others,
as a weapon for the undoing of my own kind. Instead I
walked steadily ahead.

They had depended so much on nonphysical power that
they were late in raising material weapons. I fired first,
another blast of that shocking energy, aiming above their
heads, though I longed to center it on them. But I thought
that must only be done as a last resort; those bodies must
not be destroyed.

The energy crackled, died. I realized uneasily that I had
now exhausted the laser charge. There was another cartridge

in my supply belt, but whether I would have time to recharge—

I had never believed my reaction or my senses more acute than those of most other men. But, almost without thinking, I made a swift leap to the left. Yet I did not wholly escape the menace which had crept on me from behind. An arm flung out half-tripped me. I staggered, keeping my balance only by happy chance. And I saw that Griss had crawled on hands and knees to attack. But whatever small spark of strength had supported him now failed. He collapsed again, face down—though the length of his alien body twitched and shuddered, as if muscles fought will, will flesh and bone in return.

So I edged backward at an angle to give me vision of both the three by the wall and those they possessed. There was a writhing among the latter, as if they fought to get to their feet yet could not summon strength enough. As far as I could see, those who believed themselves masters had not changed position, save that they no longer raised their hands with the round objects I suspected were weapons. Instead those arms hung limply by their sides.

Then he who wore Lidj's body toppled forward, crashing to the hard stone of the floor, making not the least attempt to save himself. And the other two followed. As they did so, that tortured movement among their slaves was stilled. I could have been standing among dead.

"Vorlund!" Foss and Borton both shouted my name so that it sounded as a single word.

I looked around to see them at the cavern entrance. And I believe they, too, thought I had fought a fatal battle. For Borton hurried forward, went down on one knee beside the inert form of Harkon, then, having laid hand on the shoulder beneath that black covering, looked to the three by the far wall.

"What did you do?"

"Used laser shock." I holstered the weapon I still held.

Foss was beside Lidj. "Dead?" he asked, but he did not look at me.

"No."

They went on to the three by the wall, stooped to turn those over so they lay on their backs. Their eyes were open, but there was no hint of consciousness. It was as if the essence of the alien personalities had withdrawn—or else—

I had gone to look at them, too. Now I wondered. Could that shock have brought about a switchover? If so—or in any case—we should have both sets of men under guard before they returned to consciousness. I said so.

"He's right." Borton, rather than Foss, backed my suggestion. He produced a tangler, used it with efficiency. First he bound the three by the wall, then he attended to those in the alien bodies, putting all the others of that band under restraint as well for good measure. In addition the three aliens were given stiff injections to keep them unconscious —or so we hoped.

We were masters now of the jack headquarters, though we put out sentries and did not accept our victory as total. There was too good a chance of others' still occupying the ship or the burrows. And the whole nature of this site was such as to make a man very wary of his surroundings, only too ready to hear strange noises, start at shadows, and the like.

We made use of the bubble in the cavern as a prison,

stowing there our blacked-out prisoners. Borton used the
jacks' com to summon the rest of his men from the
outer valley. The energy which sustain pills and E rations
had given us was ebbing. This time we did not try to bol-
ster it. Rather we took turns sleeping, eating rations we
found in the camp.

There was evidence that the jacks had been here for
some time. Signs, too, by deep flare burns left on the valley
floor, that there had been more than one ship landing and
take-off over a period of perhaps a year, or longer, planet
time. But after sleep-gas globes had made the ship ours, we
discovered very little more of the setup which had been
made to market the loot or otherwise do business off-world
—there were only faint clues for the Patrol to follow up.

Our prisoners did not revive quickly and Thanel was
loath to use medical means to induce consciousness. Too
little was known of the stresses to which they had recently
been subjected. In all there were some twenty jacks, and
the men of our own party which had been taken—including
Hunold. And our only safe control on the alien three was
to make sure they could not use their esper powers.

Thanel ordered these three, plus their alien bodies, to be
put in a separate division of the tent. There he spent most
of his waking time keeping them under observation. They
still breathed, all six of them. And the detect showed a life
signal whenever he used it on them. Yet the vital processes
were very slow, akin to the state of one in stass-freeze. And
how this state could be broken, he admitted he did not
know. After a certain time had passed he even experi-
mented by taking off his protect cap (having first stationed

a guard to watch him and move in at the first hint he might be taken over) and trying to reach them via esper means—with no result.

I had fallen asleep. And I did not know how long it was before I was shaken awake again. Foss was the one who had so abruptly roused me.

"Thanel wants you," he said tersely.

I crawled out of the pheno-bag I had found in the camp. Foss was already heading into the open where the darkness of night had largely concealed the standing ship.

But it was not the chill of the night wind probing now and then into the cavern which set me shivering as I watched him go. I have known loneliness in my life. Perhaps the worst was when I realized on Yiktor that I might never return to my human body, that it was possible I might be entrapped for years in animal form. Then I had literally gone mad, striking out into the wilderness, allowing the remnant of beast in me to take over from the human which had been transplanted. I had run, I had killed, I had skulked, I had— Today I cannot remember all that happened to me, nor do I wish to. That was loneliness.

And this—this was loneliness of another type. For in that moment when Captain Foss walked away I saw the wall which was between us. Had the building of that wall been of my doing? Perhaps, though looking back, I could not deny that given the same choices I would have done no differently. Yes, I was no longer of the *Lydis.* I could ship out on her, do my duty well, maybe better than I had a year ago. But for me she was no longer the sole home a Free Trader must have.

What had happened? I was as lost as I had been when running four-footed across the fields of Yiktor. If I was not Krip Vorlund, Free Trader born, who wanted nothing more than a berth on the *Lydis*, then who *was* I? Not Maquad—I felt no closer kinship with the Thassa than I did with the crew; even less.

I was alone! And I shuddered away from that realization, getting to my feet, hurrying to obey Thanel's summons, hoping to find forgetfulness in this task, if only for a short time.

The medic was waiting for me as I came into that inner section where the six bodies still lay on the floor, looking just as they had when I had helped to bring them in. But Thanel had the appearance of a man who had not had any rest. And to my surprise he was not alone.

Lukas, whom I had last seen lying in tangle cords, stood beside him. It was he who spoke first.

"Krip, you are the only one of us who has been through body switch. The Thassa do it regularly, do they not?"

"I don't know about doing it regularly. Anyone who wishes to train as a Moon Singer does it. But there are only a limited number of Moon Singers. And so it may not be well known to the others. They have their failures, too." My own present body was witness to that, if one was needed.

"The question is, how do they do it?" Thanel came directly to the point. "You have been through it and witnessed it done for that Maelen of yours. Do they use some machine, drug, type of hypnotism—what?"

"They sing." I told him the truth.

"*Sing!*"

"That's what they call it. And they do it best when the moon there is three-ringed, a phenomenon which only occurs at long intervals. It can be done at other times, but then it needs the combined power of quite a few Singers. And the expenditure of their energy is such that it is only tried when there is great need. The rings were fading when Maelen was transferred to Vors's body—so there had to be more Singers—"

"Maelen was a Moon Singer, *is* one," Lukas said thoughtfully.

"Her powers were curtailed by the Old Ones when she was sent into exile," I reminded him.

"All of them? The fact remains that we have body transfer here and the only other cases known are on Yiktor. It might be possible to load these"—he indicated the sleepers —"into a ship and take them there. But there is no guarantee that your Thassa would or could make the exchange. But Maelen is here—and if she knows what can be done—"

He must have seen my face then, understood to the full my reaction to what he was proposing.

"She is not an animal!" I seized upon the first argument he might be tempted to use. But how could I make him understand, he who had never seen Maelen the Moon Singer in her proper form, only as the small, furred creature who shared my cabin, whom he rated as lower than any wearing human guise—a *thing* expendable for the crew's good.

"Who said she was?" Thanel might be trying to soothe me, but I was wary. "We are merely pointing out that we do have on this planet, here and now, a being—a person who is familiar with our problem, who should be approached in the hope that we have a solution to it here, not half the galaxy away."

But the very reasonableness of his argument made it worse. I flung the truth at them.

"You take her out of stass-freeze and she dies! You"— I centered on Thanel—"saw her condition, worked to get her into stass. How long do you think she might have if you revived her?"

"There are new techniques." His low voice contrasted with the rising fury of my demands. "I can, I think, promise that I can retard any physical changes, even if her mind is freed."

"You 'think.' " I seized directly on that qualifying phrase. "But you cannot be sure, can you?" I pressed and he was frank enough to admit the truth with a shake of his head.

"Then I say 'no'! She must have her chance."

"And how are you going to give it to her? On Yiktor? What will they do for her there, even if you can get her so far? Do they have a reserve of bodies?"

Chapter 18

MAELEN

It is true that sometimes we can remember (though that memory is as thin as the early-morning mist) a way of life which is larger than ours, into which dreams or the desire to escape may lead us. Where did I roam during that time I was apart from my broken body? For it was not the nothingness of deep sleep which had held me. No, I had done things and looked upon strange sights, and I came back to the pain which was life, carrying with me an urgency that would spur me to some action I did not yet understand.

Returning, I did not see with the eyes of the body which held me now so poorly. Perhaps those eyes no longer had the power of sight. Rather did Krip's thought reach mine, and I knew he had brought about my awakening, and only in dire need.

That need worked upon me as a debt-sending, so that I knew it was one which I must answer. Tied are we always to right our debts so the the Scales of Molaster stand even!

Only with that summons came such pain of body as blotted out for a breath, or four, or six, my ability to answer.

I broke contact that I might use my strength to cut off the communication ways between my body and my mind. I did this quickly, so that pain was lulled to a point where it could be endured, remaining as only a far-off wretched wailing of a wind which had naught to do with me.

So armored, I sought Krip once more.

"What would you?"

"—body—change—"

I could not understand clearly. Body change? In me memory stirred. Body change! I was in a damaged body, one for which there was no future. A new body? How long had I existed in that other place? Time was always relative. Was I now back on Yiktor, with a new body awaiting me? Had as much time as that passed in the real world? For now it appeared that I was no longer closely tied to Krip's world, though that had once been the one I also knew best.

"Body change for whom?"

"Maelen!" Even stronger his thought-send. As if he were trying to awaken some sleeper with a shout of alarm, as does the horn man on the walls of fort keeps, where death by sword can creep out of the night unless a keen-eyed sentry sees it to give warning.

"I am here—" It would seem he had not heard my earlier answer. "What would you have of me?"

"This—" His thought became clear and he told me how it was with those of the *Lydis* and their allies.

Part of that tale was new. And, as his mental pictures built in my mind, my own remembrance sharpened. So I was drawn yet farther from the clouding mists where lately I had had my being.

Body exchange—three humans for three aliens. But—

there had been a fourth alien. A fourth! Sharply clear in my mind she suddenly stood, her hair falling about her shoulders as a dark fire cloak, and on her head— NO!

My mind-touch broke instinctively. In her crown lay the danger, an ever-present danger. But she was there—waiting —ever waiting. She could not take over any of the others, even suck their life force, since they were male—she must have one of her own sex in order to exchange. That was it! She had called me (clear was my memory now). Yet while I kept apart she could not control me, force the exchange as her kin had—force the exchange? No, that had not been her desire as I had read it last—she had wanted my life force—not my body.

"Maelen?" Krip was sensitive to my preoccupation with the woman, though he may not have known my reason. "Maelen, are you with me? Maelen!" His call was stark now with fear.

"I am here. What do you want?"

"You changed me. Can you tell us how to exchange these?"

"Am I still a Moon Singer?" I demanded bitterly. This was no proper debt, for I could not supply payment. "Is Sotrath above our heads wearing Three Rings? Where is my wand? And can animal lips, throat, bring forth the Great Songs? I am of no use to you, Krip Vorlund. Those upon whom you must call stand tall on Yiktor."

"Which means well beyond our reach. But listen, Maelen —" He began with the haste of one who has a message of importance, and then his thought wavered. But I caught what he would say. Perhaps I had known my fate from the beginning, in spite of all his efforts to save me from it.

"If you would say that this body I now wear so badly will not continue long to hold me—that I have already guessed. Have you any answer for me, since I have given one which is no help to you?"

"She—the woman of the cat crown—she is a body!"

Once more I drew upon my power, probed behind his words seeking her insidious prompting, the setting of that thought in his mind. So that was to be the method of her attack? She would use Krip to reach me with temptation. For it is very true that living creatures, offered a choice of life or the unknown ways of death, will turn to life. And in the past I think that those with whom she had had dealings were much lesser in power, so that she had grown very confident, arrogant, in her reckoning.

But I could not discover any such prompting in his mind. And I was sure he could not have concealed that from me; I knew him too well and too deeply. There was nothing there but concern and sorrow lacing around his mental image of Maelen as he had seen me on Yiktor when I had been so sure of *myself* and the powers I held.

Knowing that this was not an implanted idea, I began to consider it. I could surrender to the mist and darkness, release the anchorage which held me in this body which could not be repaired in spite of all their science. We of Molaster's people do not fear to take the White Road, knowing that this life is only the first stumbling step on a long way leading to wonders we cannot know here and now.

Yet it is also true that we *know* when the time comes for such release, and I had not received such a message. Instead there was that pattern of which I was a part and which was unfinished—of which I had been shown a glimpse. If I chose to go now out of pain, or timidity, it was not right. And so my time was not yet. But I could not remain in this body, and there was only one other—that of her who waited. For it I would have to fight, and it would be fair battle, my strength against hers; a fairer war, I believed, than she had ever fought before.

If I had had but one of the Old Ones by my side my fear would not have been so great. But this was my battle only. Had the whole rank of them stood behind me at this time I could have asked no aid from them. But where was my wand; who would sing? Suppose I entered into that waiting alien and found myself a helpless tenant—

"Maelen." Krip's call was tentative now, almost as if he only wanted to know if I could still be reached.

"Take me to the woman. Do not try to contact me again until we are there. I must conserve my strength."

Sing? I could not sing. We were not under a three-ringed moon whose glory could enhance my power. I had no one of the Thassa to stand with me. No one of the Thassa— Krip? But he was only outwardly Thassa. Yet—and now I began to consider the problem with objective concentration, as if this action did not affect me at all but dealt with others with whom I had no emotional involvement.

Exchange needed a linkage of power. Once I fronted the alien it would be my battle, but to bring her to bay I might lawfully call upon aid. There had been that dead man—or seemingly dead man—who had broadcast to keep the crew of the *Lydis* and the Patrolmen under control. He, or the will behind him, had made use not of the traditional tools of the Thassa, but of mechanical means. What one could do, could not another do also?

For long ages the Thassa have shunned the aid of machines, just as we long ago went forth from cities, put aside possessions. I knew not the way of machines. However, to say in any crisis "because I do not know this thing, it will not aid me" is to close the mind. And neither have the Thassa been given to such narrowness. Even though we withdrew from the stream of life wherein swim the plainsmen and these star travelers, we do not stagnate.

So—a machine to aid. And a machine of the *Lydis* or the Patrol that was on my side, not that of her who watched and waited. Also—she had not seen me in body. Let me be brought before her. Shock had value. And if my mind was seemingly lulled—could she so be pushed off balance, made more receptive to counterattack?

Having made my plans, I spoke to Krip again, letting him know my decision, what I would need, then as swiftly retreating once more into my safe-keeping silence, while I waited, storing up what energy I could summon. Also I must prepare for this new technique—no wand, no songs. I would instead have to funnel what power I had through a machine. But behind me would be Krip and upon him I could depend, that I knew.

Though I had shut off contact with Krip, I became aware now of mind-send. That did not come boldly and openly, but was rather like the barsk, wily, untamed, prowling at the gate of a holding, scenting the uneasy herd within, working to find the best way of breaching the barrier between it and its victims.

I wanted to explore that skulking identity, but the need in my own plan for surprise kept me back. How great an adept did I now face? I am as a little child compared to some of our Old Ones. Would I now discover that the same held true here? I could only wait for the final confrontation, and hope the machine would aid.

Though I was not aware of any change in my own surroundings, I guessed, from the increased pressure from that would-be invading mind, that I must be approaching its lair. To hold barriers on two levels of consciousness is very difficult. As I allowed that invader to edge into my—as one might term it—outer mind, I had to stage that intrusion with more care than I had ever before taken in my life. For the enemy must believe that she was succeeding in her take-over—that there were no depths beneath which I marshaled forces, prepared a counterattack.

Perhaps I reached heights that day—or night—which I had not known were possible, even for a Moon Singer. But if I did, I was not aware of my feat. I was intent only on holding the delicate balance, lulling my enemy, being ready when the moment came.

There was a sudden cessation of that cautious invasion. Not a withdrawal, but further exploration had halted. Though I could see only with the mind's eye, I saw *her!* She was there in every detail, even as Krip had showed her to me, as she had been in my dream.

That had been blurred, filtered as it had been through his reaction to her. This was as sharp and clear as the Stones of Yolor Plain where they lie in the cruel moonlight of Yiktor's midwinter. Only she did not half recline on a couch as Krip had described. Rather in this place she sat enthroned, her cloak of hair flung back to bare her body, her head a little forward as if she wished to meet me eye to eye. And the writhing cats' heads of her diadem were not in play, but all erect on their thread-thin supports, their eyes turned also upon me—watching—waiting—

Diadem! I had had my wand, through which to center my power, when I had sung the small spells and the deep ones. Even the Old Ones possessed their staffs to focus and hold the forces they controlled. Her diadem served her so.

Perhaps I erred then in revealing my sudden enlightenment. I saw her eyes narrow. The hint of a cruel twist of smile about her lips vanished. And the cats' heads—a quiver ran along their filaments, a ripple such as a passing wind brings to a field of grain.

"Maelen—ready!"

Krip broke through the shield I did not try to hold against him. I saw the cats' heads twist, turn, whirl into a wild dance. But I turned from them to join Krip's guiding thought.

By some miracle of Molaster's sending, I could follow that mind-directive. I "saw" the machine before me. Its shape, its nature were of no interest to me, only how it was to act as my wand, my own diadem. To it Krip must link me, since it was of his heritage and not of mine.

Link and hold—did he understand? He must, for the mental image of the machine was now clear and solid. I directed power to it.

Recoil—a frenzied recoil from that other—rooted in fear!

Even as she withdrew, so did my will and purpose flood behind her. Though I did not quite reach my goal. She steadied, stood firm. The diadem braced her—

Between me and my mental image of the box the cats' heads danced a wild measure. To look beyond those, focus on the box was almost too much for me. And pain—pain was beginning to gnaw once more. I could not hold the blocks I had set up in that broken body, evade the spell of the cats' heads, concentrate upon the amplifier—not all at once!

Strength feeding me—that was Krip. He could not sing where there was no true Thassa to guide him. He could only support my link with the box. And then—more—small, but holding steady. I did not know from whence that came (Molaster's gift?)—I was only glad I had it.

She had driven me back a little from the advance point I had reached. But I was still ahead of where I had begun. Look not on the cats. The amplifier—use that! Feed it with a flow of will—feed it!

A broken image—that was a flash of physical sight. Blot it out! See only what is within, not out—this battle lies within! I knew now that the ending must come quickly or else I was lost. Once more—the amplifier, call all my resources— Strike!

I broke through some intangible defense, but I allowed myself no feeling of triumph. Success in one engagement does not mean battle won. What did face me now? Almost I recoiled in turn. I had thought that what I fought was a personality, one as well-defined as I saw myself—me—Maelen of the Thassa. But this was only will; a vicious will, yes, and a dark need for domination, but still only a husk of evil left to go on running—a machine abandoned by its onetime owner, left to "live" through the mists of unnumbered years. There was no inner self wearing the diadem, just the dregs of the will and forgotten purpose. So when I broke through the shell maintained by those, I found an emptiness I did not expect. Into that space I flowed, making it my own, then barricading it against the remnant of that other.

That remnant, robo-like, was far from being vanquished. Perhaps the many years it had been in command had developed it as a form of quasi-life. And it turned on me with vicious force.

The cats! Suddenly I could see nothing but the cats, their narrow heads, their slitted eyes, crowding in upon me! They began a whirling dance around and around—the cats! They were the focus through which this thing could act!

Dimly, beyond their attempt to wall me away from the world, I could see. Not with the mental sight, no, but truly. Forms, though I found them hard to focus upon, were there. Then I knew that I was not looking through the eyes which Vors had long ago given me. I was in another body. And I realized what body that was!

The pressure on me, the waves of enmity which were as physical blows against cringing flesh—those came from the cats. I was in a body, a body which had arms—hands— I concentrated my will. And all the way that other half-presence fought me. I did not feel as if I were actually moving; I could only will it so.

Were those hands at my head now? Had the fingers tightened around the edge of the cat diadem? I set my mental control to lifting the crown, hurling it from me—

The cats' heads vanished. My vision, which had been blurred, was now vividly clear. I knew that I had a body, that I was living, breathing, with no more pain. Also—that other presence was gone as if it had been hurled away with the crown.

They stood before me, Krip, Captain Foss, strangers in

Patrol uniforms. There were others on the floor, encased in tangler cords: Lidj, Griss, the Patrol pilot—and three alien bodies.

Krip came to me, caught my two hands, looked down into my new eyes. What he read there must have told him the truth, for there was such a lighting in his face as puzzled me. I had not seen that expression before.

"You did it! Maelen, Moon Singer—you have done it!"

"So much is true." I heard my new voice, husky, strange. And I looked down upon this new casing for my spirit. It was a good body, well made, though the flow of dark hair was not Thassa.

Krip still held my hands as if he dared not let them go lest I slip away. But now Captain Foss was beside him, staring at me with the same intensity Krip had shown.

"Maelen?" He made a question of my name as if he could not believe that this had happened.

"What proof do you wish, captain!" My spirit was soaring high. I had not felt this way since I had donned fur and claws back on Yiktor.

But one of the Patrolmen cut short our small reunion. "What about it? Can you do the same for them?" He gestured to the men in bonds.

"Not now!" Krip flung at him. "She has just won one battle. Give her time—"

"Wait—" I stilled his bristling defense of me. "Give me but a little time to learn the ways of this body."

I closed off my physical senses, even as I had learned to do as a Singer, sent my inner questing here and there. It was like exploring the empty rooms of a long-deserted citadel. That which had partially animated this fortress had occu-

pied but little of it. My journey was a spreading out, a realization that I had new tools ready for my hands, some as yet
unknown to me. But there would be time to explore fully
later. Now I wished most to know how I who was Maelen
could make best use of what I had.

"Maelen!" That call drew me back. I felt once more the
warmth of Krip's grasp, the anxiety in his voice.

"I am here," I assured him. "Now—" I took full command of this new body. At first it moved stiffly, as if it had
been for long without proper controls. But with Krip's aid
I stood, I moved to those who lay in bonds, alien flanking
Terran. And their flesh was like transparent envelopes to
my sight. I knew each as he really was.

As it had been with the woman into which I had gone,
those which now occupied the Terran bodies were not true
personalities, but only motivating forces. It was strange—
by the Word of Molaster, how strange it was! I could not
have faced those who had originally dwelled therein. I
doubt if even the Old Ones could have done so. Whatever,
whoever those sleepers had been, that had once been great,
infinitely more so than the men whom only the pale remnant of their forces had taken over.

Because I knew them for what they were I was able to
break them, expel them from the bodies they had stolen.
Krip, still hand-linked with me, backed me with his
strength. And, once those aliens had been expelled, to
return the rightful owners to their bodies was less difficult.
The Terran bodies stirred, their eyes opened sane and knowing. I turned to Captain Foss.

"These wore crowns, and the crowns must be destroyed.
They serve as conductors for the forces."

"So!" Krip dropped my hand and strode across the chamber. He stamped upon some object lying there, ground his magnetic-soled space boots back and forth as if he would reduce what he trampled to powder.

In my mind came a thin, far-off wailing, as if somewhere living things were being done to death. I shivered but I did not raise hand to stop him from that vengeful attack upon the link between the evil will and the body I had won.

It was a good body, as I had known when first I looked upon it. And I found in the outer part of the chamber the means to clothe it. The clothing was different from my Thassa wear, being a short tunic held in by a broad, gemmed belt, and foot coverings which molded themselves to the limbs they covered.

My hair was too heavy and long and I did not have the pins and catches to keep it in place Thassa-fashion. So I plaited it into braids.

I wondered who she had been once, that woman so carefully preserved outwardly. Her name, her age, even her race or species, I might never know. But she had beauty, and I know she had power—though it differed from that of the Thassa. Queen, priestess—whatever— She had gone away long since, leaving only that residue to maintain a semi-life. Perhaps it was the evil in her which had been left behind. I would like to believe so. I wanted to think she was not altogether what that shadow I had battled suggested.

But the exile of that part, and of that which had animated the three male aliens, opened a vast treasure house. Such discoveries as were disclosed will be the subject for inquiry, speculation, exploration for years to come. As the jack operation (so swiftly taken over by the aliens) had been illegal by space law, those of the *Lydis* were allowed to file First Claim on the burrows. Which meant that each and every member of the crew became master of his own fate, wealthy enough to direct his life as he wished.

"You spoke more than once of treasure." I had returned to the chamber of the one in whose body I now dwelt to gather together her possessions (the company having agreed that these were freely mine), and Krip had come with me. "Treasure which could be many things. And you said that to you it was a ship. Is this still so?"

He sat on one of the chests, watching me sort through the contents of another. I had found a length of rippling blue-green stuff unlike any fabric I had ever seen, cat masks patterned on it in gold. Now they had no unease for me.

"What is your treasure, Maelen?" He countered with a question of his own. "This?" He gestured at what lay within that chamber.

"Much is beautiful; it delights the eye, the touch." I smoothed the fabric and folded it again. "But it is not my treasure. Treasure is a dream which one reaches out to take, by the Will of Molaster. Yiktor is very far away. What one may wish for on Yiktor—" What had I wished for on Yiktor? I did not have to search far in memory for that. My little ones (though I could not call them "mine" now, for I had sent them to their own lives long since). But— with little ones of their kind—a ship— Yiktor did not call me strongly now; I had voyaged too far, not only in space but somehow in spirit. Someday I wanted to go there again. Yes. I wanted to see the Three Rings of Sotrath blaze in her night sky, walk among the Thassa, but not yet. There remained the little ones—

"Your dream is still a ship with animals—to voyage the stars with your little people, showing others how close the bond between man and animal may truly become," Krip said for me. "Once I told you that you could not find treasure enough to pay for such a dream. I was wrong. Here it is, many times over."

"Yet I cannot buy such a ship, go star voyaging alone." I turned to look full at him. "You said that *your* dream of treasure was also a ship. And that you can now have—"

He was Thassa and yet not Thassa. Even as I searched his face I could see behind Maquad's features that ghost with brown skin, dark hair, the ghost of the young man I had first met at the Great Fair of Yrjar.

"You do not want to return to Yiktor?" Again he did not answer me directly.

"Not at present. Yiktor is far away, both in space and time—very far."

I do not know, or did not know, what he read in my voice which led him to rise, come to me, his hands reaching out to draw me to him.

"Maelen, I am not as I once was. I find that I am now in exile among those of my own kind. That I would not believe until here on Sekhmet it was proved. Only one now can claim my full allegiance."

"Two exiles may find a common life, Krip. And there are stars—a ship can seek them out. I think that our dreams flow together."

His answer this time came in action, and I found it very good. So did we two who had walked strange ways choose to walk a new one side by side, and I thanked Molaster in my heart for His great goodness.

Chapter 19

KRIP VORLUND

When I looked upon her who had come to me, who trusted in me (even when I had called her back to what might have been painful death, because I believed that a small chance waited for her) then I knew that this was the way of life for us both.

"Not exile," I told her. "It is not exile when one comes home!"

Home is not a ship after all, nor a planet, nor a traveling wain crossing the plains of Yiktor. It is a feeling which, once learned, can never be forgotten. We two are apart, exiled perhaps, from those who once were our kind. But before us lie all the stars, and within us—home! And so it will be with us as long as life shall last.